Watercolor Women
Opaque Men

Watercolor Women Opaque Men

A Novel in Verse

Ana Castillo

Introduction by Carmen Tafolla

CURBSTONE
NORTHWESTERN UNIVERSITY PRESS
EVANSTON, ILLINOIS

Northwestern University Press
www.nupress.northwestern.edu

Copyright © 2005 by Ana Castillo. Introduction copyright © 2017 by
Carmen Tafolla. Published 2017 by Curbstone/Northwestern University
Press. All rights reserved.

This book was originally published by Curbstone Press in 2005 with the
support of the Connecticut Commission on Culture and Tourism, the
National Endowment for the Arts, and donations from many individuals.

Printed in the United States of America

10 9 8 7 6 5 4 3 2 1

Library of Congress Cataloging-in-Publication Data
Names: Castillo, Ana, author. | Tafolla, Carmen, 1951– writer of
    introduction.
Title: Watercolor women, opaque men : a novel in verse / Ana Castillo ;
    Introduction by Carmen Tafolla.
Description: 2017 edition. | Evanston, Illinois : Curbstone/Northwestern
    University Press, 2017. | Includes bibliographical references and index.
Identifiers: LCCN 2016056399| ISBN 9780810135109 (pbk. : alk. paper) |
    ISBN 9780810135116 (e-book)
Subjects: LCSH: Mexican American women—Poetry. | Working mothers—
    Poetry. | Single mothers—Poetry. | LCGFT: Narrative poetry.
Classification: LCC PS3553.A8135 W38 2017 | DDC 811/.54—dc23
LC record available at https://lccn.loc.gov/2016056399

For the women along the U.S.–Mexican border, this side and the other. For women on borders everywhere, geographical and otherwise. And for the opaque men in their lives, striving to understand. For their courage, each and every one.

Contents

Watercolor Women Opaque Men as a novel in verse began to germinate years before it took root. If I were to pinpoint the precise influence, time, and place, it would have been reading a copy of *Helen in Egypt* by the poet Hilda "H.D." Doolittle that I found at a university bookstore not long after graduate school. As a self-taught writer, my training has come exclusively from my reading. However, it wasn't until decades later, when I set upon an epic literary journey of my own, that H.D.'s example came back to me. Unlike Helen, a legendary figure of monumental proportions, the beauty in my story would be of humble origins and anonymous.

The protagonist *Ella,* her name a gesture toward the translated pronoun "she," initially rose in my imagination one fine summer afternoon in my hometown of Chicago. For some time, my attention had been focused on prose. I have found the explorations of writing prose and poetry to be very different. Prose necessitates a conscious planning out of a narrative; a certain focus is required to follow a plot and subplots. Poetry, with its demands on language, imagery, and cosmic connections throughout world history, requires faith. The poet must trust in her instincts in order to illuminate for the reader something about the human experience that is both unique to her skill and her knowledge and yet universal.

The summer of 2003 during which a poem became a book was a season of quiet reflection and solitude in my native city of Chicago. That year, an editor who was preparing an updated edition of my early collection of poetry, *My Father Was a Toltec,* asked whether I happened to have anything recent to include. In fact, I had drafted out a rather long, and perhaps grim, poem, which was neatly filed in hard copy in a cabinet and nearly forgotten. I decided to work on it, and since I was,

I think, in a better mood than when I first wrote it, I chose to revise and uplift it from its sad tone. It is fine to write sad poems, but it was the only new poem I was going to add to the collection, and I didn't feel that the tone represented my attitude toward life in those years.

It is not uncommon for my novels to start first as short stories, and something similar happened here. Storytelling came fluidly in verse when I'd set out simply to revise a poem. I became interested in the character of Ella and wanted to know her backstory. Thus came a second poem and then a third, and so on. Before I knew it, six weeks had gone by and I was still writing. It was about then that I decided to wrap up what had become, I believe, an epic telling of the enigmatic character that first came to me one night in a few verses. The poems that would become *Watercolor Women Opaque Men* were inspired entirely by the subject—Ella, everywoman. Ella rose out of the most unassuming of circumstances; indeed, countless migrant workers throughout U.S. history may share moments of her story. Yet whether as an artist, a kind of self-styled urban warrior, or both, Ella fits within the grandeur of the universe just as the unnamed stars shine within the constellations.

ACKNOWLEDGMENTS

First, I extend *mis gracias sinceras* to the Curbstone family for believing in poetry like bread. To sustain confident balance on a tightrope one requires a reliable net. For their valued support and friendship I would like to thank the following esteemed individuals: *las sabias* medicine women, Clarissa Pinkola-Estes, Martha Medrano, Teresa Ramos, and, especially, Susan Bergholz. I was falling, falling, but I am indebted to *mis amigos veteranos* in the arts *y la vida*: Juana Guzmán, Rina García, and Carlos Cumpian, whose love made sure it never happened. Not least of all, day and evening, our beloved family pet, El Rick, is remembered for taking me out on our daily walks to the beach and all over our neighborhood under gentrification, in memoriam.

Last, but most important, I thank the visitation of the gods and my ancestors for bringing me their stories while on this earth. To all: I hope these verses are worthy of their trust.

Introduction: The Larger Canvas

Carmen Tafolla

Ana Castillo's *Watercolor Women Opaque Men* is both entrancing and enlightening, a poignant and eagle-eyed exposure of society's multiple tools of oppression for brown, low-income women caught in the web of poverty, sexism, racism, and a system that denies the full expression of an individual's talent or passions. This is the breathless and mysterious tale of a gutsy young woman trying to survive the contemporary world while strengthened, informed, and also sometimes burdened by layers of family and personal history. The heroine is very much in touch with her past and her family, though not controlled by them, and she struggles to find her own path forward, despite the many obstacles that working-class women of color encounter. This novel in verse is not painted in a broad swath of generic colors—dull and tired blacks and whites and blues—but instead in all the excitement and gritty detail of contemporary life, lifting us off the page and outside the book to the full-color scenery of today's reality. The novel is, indeed, painted onto the larger canvas of life, and therein lies its strength and its potency to speak to us on multiple levels of consciousness.

In *Watercolor Women Opaque Men* Ana Castillo has created a masterpiece of Latina identity and self-empowerment and has given expression to mythic images of colossal strength alongside the dredgings of pus, mud, and sexism. She explores the sweaty underbelly of the Chicano experience in the United States, ranging from the injustices of workers without papers and without rights to the invisibility of Latino contributions to this nation:

How the *coyotes* pack us like sardines

In death traps on wheels.
How they leave us wandering in the desert
like deranged Jews

Searching for the Promised Land.
No, that's us.
The one-celled organisms

At the bottom of the food chain
That nevertheless—
Oh,

Not for a minute,
should anyone be mistaken,
that it is not us—

Who have made this country
what it is.   (123)

Reflecting a strong sense of historical process, Castillo conveys elements of the long-neglected and suppressed history of the Indo-Hispanic peoples whose presence here preceded the existence of the United States. She also portrays the incredible strength of a Latina at the bottom of society's prestige ladder who defiantly pursues her liberation and her actualization, crossing lines, mores, and expectations to transform and grow and claim her own power.

Mestizaje and Duality

In her aesthetically crafted epic poem, Castillo follows this personal transformation while also plumbing the depths of *motivos* and yearnings for a dozen characters, both male and female. She reveals them in all their idiosyncratic plumage and psychological contradiction, making connections between people that expose them as different facets of the same being. Like the duality of the Omecihuatl/Ometecuhtli, the Aztec god of creation, male and female are two halves of the same body, and the human experiences outlined here are all tied together in the experience of one life. This book is the essence of *mestizaje*, a blended world of opposing root cultures, where the reader finds both Allah and "Für Elise," both Fun with Phonics and a *temazkal* sweat lodge, both Our Lady of Guadalupe and Elvis, as in the lives of millions of *mestizo* bicultural Latinos, taking from the mythologies and experiences of different cultures to craft their own survival instructions:

> when Berkeley still belonged to the Socialists
> and San Jose was a sleepy Mexican town.

> . . .

> And when a poet walked in
> you'd think it was Elvis *Live*.
> So there I was, a young mother

> With my child flung over the
> left hip, the bow over the right
> shoulder because

> You'd never know.
> Amazons were always on call . . .

> . . .

in the Machu Picchu version
of Amazonian legacy.   (77–79)

This texture of cultural experiences from different legacies and different centuries creates a distinct and very diverse world, one that weaves *mestizaje* into every moment and *restores* a deeper reality by *re-story-ing* our human interactions. The final result is not only one characterized by *mestizaje* and duality, but also by a deep *respeto* for all beings, even heifers wishing "to catch moonlight."

But what can be said of heifers grazing

Spoiled as they are,
with udders that hang so low
and long for so much.

Wishing their hooves could extend
themselves to catch silver moonlight,
but never can?   (236–37)

Like *Borderlands: The New Mestiza* (1987), the deeply significant book by Gloria Anzaldua about what it means to live between nations, between languages and cultures, between traditional genders, and between the narrow expectations of traditional and oppressive expectations, Castillo's work develops the concept of *mestiza* (mixed-race) consciousness; also like *Borderlands*, this work presents Chicanas as complex characters living in two worlds, speaking two languages, and being capable of more than a single-minded heterosexual inclination. In keeping with the Navajo cultural and linguistic affirmation of four genders, the world painted in *Watercolor Women* reveals the voices of individuals of different sexual preferences (women who like men, women who like women, men who like women, and men who like men). And in characteristic Castillo fashion, no lines are absolute, no categories exclusive. Characters wander between these categories, sometimes overlapping, sometimes staying with a single preference, sometimes changing, sometimes pushing preference into the domain of dominance. The hegemony of male dominance is complicated by ethnic and economic biases, and the characters revealed become as complex and difficult to stereotype as humans are in actuality, thus creating a realistic portrayal of the human character. Unlike *Borderlands*, *Watercolor Women* develops these concepts and decolonizes history over the trajectory of a dramatic novel boiling with the realities of abuse, patriarchy, and economic oppression within one life.

Concientización and Ella's Trajectory

In *Watercolor Women Opaque Men*, Castillo exposes the bare realities of a young mother cleaning toilets in order to support her son and gain her freedoms. The novel magnifies the development of feminism and humanism polished through the echoes of family history, as when a steely Mamá Grande, in the middle of *La Revolución*, survives both physically and spiritually by working in a saloon and eating grubs and cactus. These echoes of family stories are not used as decoration or as colorful metaphors and mythologies, but as a concrete part of our protagonist's daily life and strategies. They are an essential part of how she views and analyzes the world. This is a novel grounded in the material condition of a contemporary society quite comfortable in its deep grooves of oppression and its quotidian ruts of inhumane practices and policies. The protagonist projects a confident *concientización*, that critical consciousness that emphasizes not only acquiring an understanding of the world and its social and political injustices, but also taking action against the oppressive elements in one's life that have been illuminated by that awareness. While the original Portuguese term *conscientizacão*, popularized by Brazilian educational theorist Paulo Freire, has been used worldwide in analyzing situations of social injustice, Latino groups in the United States and throughout the Americas have embraced the Spanish term *concientización* as that consciousness-raising fully cognizant of the history and current situation of Latinas and Latinos in society, as well as how they and other ethnicities, classes, and gender identities have figured into the power structures of those societies. But even Ella's unflinching *concientización* is not enough to offset the severity of the categories stacked against her—female, Latina, dark-skinned, poor, and, yes, aware of her own capacities, her own dignity, and her own right to receive a respect she rarely encounters in her work and school environments.

This Chicana protagonist, appropriately and significantly named *Ella*, the Spanish word for "she," is fully aware of her family and personal history, and of the contradictions and injustices that she has experienced and inherited. She is able to echo and comprehend the best of their philosophical and emotional resources and to eschew and denounce the worst. But more important, she is able to ride the line between these two areas, and draw the best *from* the worst. This is most dramatically portrayed in the moment when her great-grandmother, carefully de-licing and braiding her great-grandchild's long hair while recounting tales of her own independence and commitment to self-sufficient survival, suddenly and without anyone's permission chops off the treasured braid and hands it to the girl as a monetary resource and a message of the harsh strength and self-sufficiency she will need in order to survive. Despite her shock and her innocence, the girl is aware of the power of the spoken lesson, punctuated by an irreversible action that could, she understands, possibly save her independence. Her mother says:

"Just know the law
and know what is yours.
Know your worth."

Then, without having asked,
made an announcement,
requested the father's permission,

Or even wondered if the girl would have consented,
Mamá Grande cut the braid with her
sewing scissors.

With a sharp *zas*,
unrecoverable and no way to retract,
gone just like that.

"Here," Mamá Grande said,
handing over the severed tresses,
"One day you'll need a few pesos.

"You can sell this.
When all accounts are made,
you will always be your most reliable resource." (29–30)

The reality of abuse, oppression, and constrained lives is portrayed in clear contrast to the feminism espoused by such earthshaking figures of womanhood as Mamá Grande, who with yanks of hair and raps on the head instructs; checks for lice; shares personal history and the politics of the Revolution;

and deftly commits bold, harsh, and irreversible actions defined by her guiding *consejo*, words of advice that the protagonist will never forget. Mamá Grande's profound analysis of all the changes with regards to women's status—before, during, and after the Revolution—powerfully underlines the message: *Your worth is inside you; you are the one on whom you will most be able to count.*

This is a novel critical to the understanding of strength in spite of multiple oppressions. It is a song of *concientización* and a feminist proclamation of the value of the self, whether one's uniqueness fits the expectations of others' traditions and stereotypes or not.

The book is simultaneously a documentation of a life in process and a declaration of protest evolving into transformative grace. Its feminist and humanist stance grows steadily stronger despite the onslaught of blows, and this stance reaches a clarity that comes from the big picture, the larger canvas of perspective gained from years of experience at all levels of the economic structure. An important part of building this internal strength despite the blows is the "calling out" of the oppression, the naming of it in a way that refuses to blame the victim. In the following poem, a child born into this world wants to will away his own destiny and knows he is capable of rising above it, while feeling the suffocation of the powers and structures that work against him:

> To the ancient ones
> *Tonalli*
> meant a child came into this world
>
> With his own destiny.
> But even so, a man could will it away,
> rise above or fall below.

The problem was
That destiny was all around
and suffocating.   (122)

The trajectory itself is as realistic as the double-shift life of the low-income Latina worker. This difficult life is one in which no deus ex machina descends from the sky to rescue her. She is, as Mamá Grande predicted, her own most reliable resource. And that is why she *must* grow this incredible internal strength if she is to survive; that is why she names the oppression, calls it out, rejects it, and becomes her own feminist, humanist, and nontraditional pillar of strength.

While this powerful novel in verse is constantly remembering and integrating its history and the possible outcomes of each situation, it also moves steadily and powerfully forward like an inevitable force of nature. Although Ella is confronted with economic and personal stumbling blocks and slapped down by institutions and societal expectations, she keeps developing her power at a recognizable and steady pace. Like its protagonist, the novel moves stubbornly forward, standing firmly in a chronological present that merely absorbs and digests the past, using it as a source of fuel: "I hung on / . . . / I / refused / to forget" (87–88).

Toward the end of the book, the protagonist finally finds herself in a utopian setting because she has helped discover and create this oasis and has reached it through her own maturity. But even the "utopia" where "They live for the fiestas, / grind corn bare-breasted, / Let gay sons wear dresses, / Everyone has a job and a place / and the women / run it" (200) becomes the place of pain, near-death, and eventual resurrection to her increased spiritual power and freedom.

One of the great and undecorated beauties of this novel in verse is its sheer range—no limits, no constraints, but the whole range of life, tragedy, passion, grief, exposure, betrayal, resurrection, incest, childrearing, child liberation, love between women and men, women and women, men and men, women and themselves, institutions and cruelty, mythology and the mundane. But all of these themes are interwoven and carefully planned, not spilled on the page in random succession. They unfold like a bud, poetically revealing itself and growing to its full bloom of maturity a self-empowered beauty that sheds the unwanted abuses like "A meteorite in the sky, / nothing but a flashing light / for a second or two" (36). The portrait of the oppressions is gracefully painted on a much bigger canvas— the tale of the other self, of Ella, the woman in development, the woman to be. And this, not the cumulative impact of the oppressions, is where the thematic purpose is revealed. The growth of the self and the process of self-empowerment are viewed both internally and externally, throughout the mirrors of time, in contrast to the supporting characters and incidental characters, and from an almost omniscient voice. Ella, this watercolor woman, is explored through many points of her challenges and development, and she is finally allowed to claim her right to self-actualization. Ella is allowed to fully bloom in all the colors of her experience and strength.

Tripartite Layers of Meaning: A Pattern of Threes

As a novel in triplicate levels, *Watercolor Women Opaque Men* is characterized by a profound understanding of the pre-Columbian mythologies, the classical Greek mythology, and the intimate life of low-income Latina women working in a world that contains wealthy penthouses, the Gap, Spanish-language television, and a nominally Christian United States. Laced throughout with an Aztec mythology that calls on the powers of Ometecutli and Omecihuatl, the male and female progenitors of life, this immediacy of the pre-Columbian Creation and Destruction stories threatens us as we walk through these pages and this life. The sound of the words, from whichever linguistic origins they come, breathes smoothly through the poetic lines, blending and folding between English, Spanish, and Nahuatl: "Not so much as the wind–/ the formidable *Ehecatl*–/ was permitted to touch her boy" (99).

In this world of the transnational/transcultural worker where nations, languages, and opposite economic levels live symbiotically, the jaws of Xolotl, the child's entrance into this world with his own Tonalli destiny, and the new fire ceremonies and rites to the sun are all present and visible to those who can see. But these pre-Columbian icons coexist with Demeter, Medusa, Osiris and Ra, Kaumari, and also Jonah and Jesus. This simultaneity allows these cultures and their myths to be deconstructed from the perspective of those who work at their foundation, bearing the weight of all the hierarchies above them.

There is a swift and accurate carving here of images on three levels, perfectly translated and coordinated between cultures, a haunting reflection of the multiculturalism in which low-income, language-minority women live and work.

> But the mother,
> Oh, the mother
> never stopped.

> Part Medusa,
> part Mother Goose,
> and part Xochiquetzal: (100)

Underlining this echo of threes, the poetic structure of Castillo's novel glides smoothly and compellingly forward in tercets, three-line verses that move ahead like some unstoppable force with great determination. The broken line between verses driving us always forward, accelerating the speed, increasing the suspense, and when they do stop unbroken within a verse, bringing finality and force to the ending.

> A fuchsia sun froze in the sky in midday.
> Wild *urracas* laughed in the distance.
> Everything stayed away
>
> Until he died.
> And when he did, *Ella* came,
> tho' she couldn't say why.   (38)

A Shape-shifting Voice, and Earthshaking Figures of Herstory

The novel begins with an exquisite *ella*, "she," the other, the self, the reflection, the seed, and this striking stance away from the self becomes a literary tool, allowing a dual perspective on the voice of the protagonist. The opening poem, *"Ella,"* moves the reader along a decoy trajectory: a reference to a woman recalled by an old friend. Immediately, the reader begins to wonder whether this recalled woman is the speaker in the poem. Memories of a friend who is in trouble resonate in a more sophisticated presentation. Is "she" a *She* or an *I* speaking? "I wonder where that woman went / who stretched illusions / like fingertips toward the sky and farther yet" (3).

The narrative stance implies that the watercolor woman has a haunting significance; she is both full of color and yet somehow translucent, not burdened by heavy-layered paints that block out the colors below. This woman "who stretched illusions" later appears repeatedly as Ella, and she utilizes both dimensions (first and third person) to brilliantly express a depth of being (both a being and a recollection of being)—the woman from today studying the woman from long ago and finding herself in the process. This removal of the self from the analysis in order to better understand the woman the self has become is a powerful and suspenseful tool in the telling of the tale, and it allows the novel to unravel breath by breath, in subtle revelations, until the full bloom of the woman is actualized in a magnificent resolution at the end of the novel.

There is an epic grandeur here. In "Lord and Lady of Sustenance," the protagonist traces her own conception, "not in the backseat of a Studebaker . . .":

> but on a lumpy sack of garlic heads
>
> That they had picked by sundown,
> and which felt like the hump of an alligator.
> She would swear forever—
>
> . . .
>
> that is what broke her back
> and not *la pizca*—   (8)

This is a grandeur dressed in burlap and suffused with the daily life of laborers, expressed in all the eloquence of Aztec mythology. And while Ella fled the stories, did not bury the progenitors "or show up at their funerals, / long gone—like a gazelle" (10), their mythology has pervaded her life and left her knowing that these stories of Ometecutli and Omecihuatl "took turns trying to make them/us forget: / The day in the fields, / the bushels we filled by quota, / calluses on our cracked little hands . . ." (11).

The Lord and Lady's grandeur lies not in a material castle but in the strength of a stubborn survival and in the depth of their love for each other.

They were, without doubt, made for each other,
like a trunk that got split by a ray of lightning,

With roots extending deep
down, beneath the earth, that entwine
and speak to each other in silence

Unable to extract,
no matter droughts or rains.   (18)

The use of the narrator's voice to reflect and dimensionalize
Ella's voice and concerns adds a strange and haunting distance
to this very intimate tale. The objective eye, the heart cooled
by the high winds of clarity and distance far above the heat of
proximity and passion—this is the third person observing Ella,
narrating coolly but with a broad view of what happens and
what can happen from nation to nation and decade to decade,
with metaphors and mythologies interlayered with the grace
of maturity and wisdom. This is not merely *ella*, an "I" dressed
in "she" camouflage, but a power from a higher, more omni-
scient dimension, the voice of a homegrown power that comes
from scars and knocks and the wisdom of years of living with
no resources beyond those of one's own making.

At other points, the power of womanhood appears in all
its bloodiest and most threatening forms, augmenting its
power in sometimes monstrous ways, as in "*Cipactli*: Woman
as Monster," where "I am a colossal toad with mouths / at all
my joints / dripping blood" (31). But the claiming of self, of
different halves of the self as one, is repeatedly reaffirmed as
Ella searches through friends, lovers of both sexes, heroes and
sheroes, employers and teachers, and plunges wholeheartedly
into different mythologies and memories and time projections
to find out, "Who is this *she*?"

Perhaps the most delightful of these earthshaking woman figures appears in "*La Amazona* (or, The Eighties in San Francisco)," where Castillo's mastery of character and profound eloquence of human spirit lay bare the strength of women. Here, both genders dare to defy traditional roles with endearing affection and connection across the lines set for them by society: "He adored / The masculine / in a woman / the feminine / In men. / We are all / one of each" (74–75). Castillo is superb in the portrayal of three- and four-dimensional characters whose lives she traces effortlessly, yet profoundly. While unexpected outcomes abound amidst bold reaffirmations of life, freedom is defined in simple terms: "and we went on / For a time like that, / feeling free, / which is all you can do / When you talk about / freedom, / is to feel it" (76). Amidst commentary on the sons of Amazons ("Boys . . . raised / by Amazons . . . / Were bound / to know that a woman / was not to be fooled with" [79]) and the inherent humor of layering a modern San Francisco with Amazonian mythology ("Amazons were always on call" [78]), there is an abundance of rich and speculative imagery. Even historical conquests are redefined in this resurrection of an Amazonian feminism. But the most telling of the precepts lies hidden in this eleven-page poem's introductory pages: "Without evidence / there is no history. / But we could invent / her story, / we could make us she . . ." (73–74). Castillo gives us the universal reflection, the multifaced mirror in these powerful lines, allowing us to both appreciate the severity of the whitewashing of HIS-story in the disappearance of the conquered or disempowered from the pages of the texts, and to envision the possibilities for re-creation of the self: "*Soy Ella—la Otra / who once was / whole*" (32).

A renewed, reinvigorated herstory arises here: "The Great Incas might / have won had they taken / the women / Into knighthood / And not as their mistresses" (79). But for all of the *Amazona*'s ability to pull out a man's eye or cut off his thumbs, the harshest blow comes in the parting lines, when she wonders if "Mamá Grande was right / about the Y chromosome" (81). This summary implication that to have a Y chromosome–to be male–is not an asset to a woman but a liability, echoes like a haunting whisper from Mamá Grande's own experiences that told her not to count on men but on herself, and it flies in the face of the teachings of centuries of male-dominated cultures.

Feminism becomes a tool for the actualization of humanity, for the telling of a more complete story.

> *Ella escribió su propia elegía.*
> It's not at all what anyone wants to do.
> As if one could without premeditation.
>
> But we can–she and I.
> the one left to remember
> and the one free to die.   (238)

The denouement of this book lies in its final six poems (some fifty-two pages in all) that bring the reader to a sense of resolution and respite. In the first of these six poems, Ella arrives to a tropical and festive paradise where women are allowed to be boisterous and bare-breasted and to run the place, "Not with the air of a queen, / but with the purpose and authority / of Secretary of State" (201). In this idyllic and feminist-indigenous haven, women and men are true and equal partners in society. The past is not erased but remembered:

> A red stain
> reminder on the forehead–
> not Hindu, flower of the trumpet vine or hippy tattoo,

But vestige
of when they were
branded.   (202)

This symbol of the branded forehead is not a whimsical met-
aphor but rather an accurate reflection of the early Spanish
colonial era in Mexico, when Indian women were branded on
their foreheads, enslaved, and forced to carry bags of silkworm
eggs under their breasts as human incubators. Instead of wip-
ing away heritage, the people of this isthmus have utilized it
as a tool for empowerment, cultural memory, and liberation.

While feminist themes in the novel are consistent through-
out, it is significant that when the resolution of this story
finally begins to unfold and life begins to come together with
all the features visible, it happens within the context of a fem-
inist society. "A Night Without Stars on the Isthmus" takes
the reader to a new place emotionally, and it pulls into a tan-
gible form a feminist society with welcome changes from the
world in which Ella has lived before. The reader has already
learned that this watercolor painting is neither a whitewash-
ing of women's innocence nor a condemnation of men. As
stated in an earlier poem, "Not only men / were / assholes"
(86).

Opaque Men

The novel has more than a few surprises, and some of these
are in the revelation of male characters such as Matías in "Ton-
alli," who are viewed initially in the third person and then later
in the first person. While the spotlight usually moves around
Ella, sometimes it swivels and turns the fullness of its light on
the lives and backgrounds of characters who were previously

seen as incidental and minor. Matías's voice is given depth and history in a fifteen-page poem that details his escape from a homeland where "Even the air is violent / and the sky wretched, / The earth, once fertile, / . . . fallow where there / isn't asphalt" (125). We begin to appreciate the wisdom and sensitivity of this old soul in a young body as he describes his role in the societies he came from and to, with a profound understanding of the role he serves "At the bottom of the food chain" (123).

The men's motivations, failings, and dreams are plumbed with authenticity and told with the voices of their own realities. Yet they are opaque, a word that speaks of non-transparency, clouds, blurriness, or being impenetrable to light; not allowing light to pass through. In the context of this novel, opacity may be expressed by a male "thickness" that is neither as flexible nor as compliant as what light and understanding represent. This book presents many instances in which rays of understanding and connection, *comadrazgo*, collaboration, and brilliance come from the female figures, and where men represent a different dynamic or physics in response to light. They absorb it, but do not let it flow through them. They redefine it, but do not reveal it.

Perhaps the most revealing of these opaque men is Rodrigo Reyes, Ella's friend, twin "partner in crime," gay confidante, and the only one allowed to ask her the piercing questions that she would claw out anyone else's eyes for asking. It becomes part of her search for a personal identity and a sexual identity that she can study this male reflection with his own dark secrets against the light of her own being and conclude that, with his friendship and encouragement, "he carried my pouch / of sharpened arrows" and that "He counted / On my aim" (77). This friend does not fear, denigrate, or criticize her role as an "*Amazona*" but instead calls her by that name "as an endearment" (74).

A subtle contrast to this twin study in an opaque man is a reflection in "Lunar Twin," where Ella encounters another woman so like her, but younger, thinner, almost a mirror of an earlier time: A "doppleganger– / who slipped through the fifth dimension" (191). A lover? A sister? And then, upon discovering that the woman paints with watercolors just as she does, the resemblance becomes too overpowering and Ella exits in a rush:

> pushed the elevator button hard,
>
> Pounded it with your fist,
> until you realize she has not
> come after you.   (196)

This twin is then revealed to be not an opaque reflection but rather a watercolor woman, someone so close to who she is that the similarities are unsettling. Because the penetration of light through a doppelganger can dazzle and even blind her, confuse her with what belongs to her and what belongs to her twin, she must run; she must escape. In contrast, because her other twin is male, his twinship becomes an alliance, not a confusion between who he is and who she herself is. He absorbs her light and maintains his opacity. The lunar twin, though, softens the lines between herself and Ella like layers of watercolors, revealing what is below. The lines between them disappear, threatening their separate existence.

Word Choice, Style, Language, and a Transporting Metaphor

Exquisite and beautifully crafted, *Watercolor Women Opaque Men* is filled with messages and metaphors that are liquid and translucent, in sharp contrast to the opacity of the men described in the title. The story is fully elaborated in language that is short, effortless, and serious as blood.

Ella se puso a grabar cada detalle
like a lithograph,
a detective for future mapping.

She started with Mamá Grande's soft hands,
like crushed orchids,
pale and brown-spotted.   (22)

Castillo's word choice is compact but eloquent, with just enough
metaphor to transport the reader into the realm of the novel.

You can forget everything
about your life
when you ride the train.

It goes underground,
then comes up into the light.
You watch what used to be

Back porches, laundry lines,
defunct refrigerators, junk stashed and piled high
and are now still back porches

But disguised as furnished decks
Complete with barbecue pits
And flower boxes with geraniums.   (53)

. . .

He stared not at her eyes,
that her lovers would say later,
when she'd have them,

Had the depth of caves.   (58)

This liquidity of language continues in "A Night Without Stars on the Isthmus," a poem in which the metaphors are as natural as the scenery: "*Ella* smiling in her half-sleep / rocking in the welcome breeze / like a ripened fruit on a branch" (211). Within the context of this idyllic isthmus and emotional respite, the metaphor slips as smoothly into the story as a sliver of light. Yet Castillo's metaphor and imagery change characteristically in an instant to fit the voice and tone of each character, losing none of the appropriateness but reflecting different personalities as adeptly as a one-woman dramatic show. In the poem "The Seminarian," Castillo captures "the doubt of the lonely man, / draped like a vest of horse hair, / that chafed and bled the flesh" (159) followed by his sudden awareness

of *her*—

A wash
of dusk rose and aquamarine
on coarse *amate* paper—

Casually at first, he noticed
her, a stone
along his labyrinthine walk—   (160)

The metaphor is neither overdone and forced nor underutilized and dull but rather minimalist and natural, effortlessly evolving to build the intricacies and depth of each character. It reflects the voice, perspective, images, and mind-patterns of the character being painted onto this canvas of a life of acquaintances: "He pampered her. He was compassionate / when she menstruated, / Folded into an accordion with cramps" (69). Often, the metaphors reflect the life-growth of the protagonist, allowing the reader to see, feel, and experience the full and powerful impact of the novel as one would experience a life, growing deeper and more mature until it fully develops.

The style Castillo uses is polished by her years of masterful word-crafting; not an extra adjective or useless adverb clutters these pages. In her concise and vivid word choice, nouns and verbs do the heavy lifting, and the power of the actions and relationships is enough to seize our attention without ornate descriptions or decorations: "Lose the dead weight / if you're going to fight. / It's in the manual" (78). Each of her words and each of the images carries its potency and engraves itself on our skin and in our hearts with no need of further fanfare.

An eloquent mastery of two languages (sometimes three or four) in complicity creates new forms not possible within the limits of one language. "It did not cross their thick cabeza-heads / that such a woman just might not like / to see herself or be thought of as a victim" (147). This is an example of how the image of their "heads" can be made even thicker, more dimwitted, and slower to comprehend by becoming "cabeza-heads," a compound word built on *cabeza*, the Spanish word for "head," and the English word *heads*. How dimwitted can they be to neither get it through their heads nor through their *cabezas*? The combination of languages maximizes the power of each in unexpected ways, slowing down the situation in this instance, speeding up or underscoring it in another.

The rhythm of *Watercolor Women*'s phrases is melodic and deft, without hesitation, and it dances gracefully from one concept to the next, taking the fewest possible steps:

> Put a name to her
> so by the curve of her calf,
> slope of her hip,
>
> Hollow of her waist,

length of her neck
down to the collarbone

As she turns to you
in her sleep—
you know you exist

Apart from her.   (185)

These lines from "Lunar Twin" are not the exception where
Castillo's verse is concerned. They are typical of the grace
of her sentence fluency. Indeed, the sentence fluency is like
a liquid, running and filling all spaces to an equal depth. The
sentences are varied enough to sound like a sequence of songs,
but they are songs that have especially poetic lyrics:

She swallowed the sumptuous neck bone
of a turtle hidden
in *Sandunga stew*.

Sandunga was not an exotic
dish or a spice
but a robust woman,

Skin, the color of bark,
y frondosa
like a leafy tree with a wide trunk,   (199)

Resolution and Revelation

While the mythological references, thematic issues, sentence
length and style, and directness of humor in *Watercolor Women*

Opaque Men run to the most adventurous ends of the gamut, there is no variation in literary quality, a standard hard to achieve in a novel in verse. Even in culminating moments of action or tragedy, the images are sharp, the words sparse, the forward movement compelling, and the metaphor a fluid fit, as in the following lines from "A Night Without Stars on the Isthmus" at the denouement of the book:

> No one noticed
> when she fell
>
> Just as the world has never
> Noticed
> When she stood.
>
> She fell by the crude wooden table,
> like a morsel of *tamal,*
> sniffed at by stray dogs, stepped on by dancing feet.   (205–6)

The unexpected turn that has her dying in this glorious isthmus seems, at first, a parable on the contemporary American street metaphor for happiness: "I thought I'd died and gone to heaven." But the asphyxiation on the bone is real enough to have her observing her end and exploring "the trap door that opened / at the end of all the hells of Mitlan" (204) as she slowly dies.

With the *Sandunga* savior pulling the bone from her throat, she drifts off into something stranger than her resurrection, and "Her paintings, / Crude yet pure expressions of herself, / As they had always been, / came to her head" (208). These four hundred and two paintings, "numbered and named" (209) parade neatly before her "like four hundred stars / in indigo *cielos*" (210). And this *Mimixcoa* collection of her paintings allows the reader to know that all the characters, all the beings with whom *ella*, "she," has interacted in this lifetime, were paintings and expressions of herself.

The poem concludes with her awareness, despite public disapproval or pity, that these paintings, these self-portraits, will be publicly shown, for:

> She had nothing to hide
> or to apologize about.
>
> She had died once
> and once was enough
> to know she could die
>
> And that would be that,
> but she could not return
> and live without stars.   (212–13)

The deepest resolution in this novel of introspection and interaction is this blending of realities, human faces, and voices into one diamond displaying its facets as if they are dreams. The resolution creates one larger canvas upon which are displayed the many portraits of being, expressed at different points of time and desire, and in different bodies, genders, and mythologies. The story is a conquest of the limitations of mortality and singleness, an overlaying of watercolors onto a canvas that displays areas of opacity and areas of light. In the final analysis, *Watercolor Women Opaque Men* reveals the beauty and the power of life.

**Watercolor Women
Opaque Men**

I. *Ella*

An old friend recalled a woman
who sent letters from afar.
She once painted envelopes

With watercolors
of palm trees and seashores,
sealed them with a lipstick kiss.

Now, two days past
the last full moon
and that conversation,

I wonder where that woman went
who stretched illusions
like fingertips toward the sky and farther yet.

She no longer wrote,
was never good with the telephone.
But might a voice,

tho' small yet clear
call out from deep
inside one's breast?

Would it tell who loved
that Watercolor Woman best,
if ever anyone at all?

I knew her as a girl,
common as the rows of artichokes she picked,
skin burnt like roasted almonds,

But more or less clever in a city dress.
It disturbs me (as it did then),
how many disguises

A female in bloom must pretend
to defend the green bough that she is before each wind.
To recall the bars, dim lighting and cigarettes,

The fact that there are always too many women
with dreams that hang like cheap baubles from soft earlobes,
wrapped around a soon-to-fade neck.

An excess of feminine humanity;
such that they distress the rest of us
who only want to live

And die,
and what happens throughout life
is God's prerogative.

(Oh God.
Did I really just
say that?)

She died, I heard.
Well, of course.
They all do, as each of us will in our time.

But this one took something of mine.
She was not a thief.
She took it without knowing.

Sometimes, I go
from room to room looking.
But it hasn't turned up.

Serves me right, I guess.
I only wish
that she had loved me less.

II. The Gods Come Together

The gods convene in *Tamoanchan*,
a place where you cannot return.
They dance and delight over the newly dead.

They carve flutes and pipes from their bones
as they deliberate over
the women who loved women,

The men who loved men,
and all those who never loved at all.
The gods are adroit enough.

One can't dispute that much.
But they do get bored.
And so cause the disruption

Of a certain flow of events
that otherwise would have made it easy
for everyone to go to heaven.

They roll oranges in the aisles,
tickle feet while we sleep.
Like a phantom, a vision, one more illusion

They put before us a woman *de aquarela*
whom we do not know
and never will know

Who bestows us with her smile
and that smile
breaks us in half.

In search of such a glance again
we would let our children go begging in the streets.
Oh—

Don't dare say that it isn't so,
that only the indecent have such thoughts.
At some point

All the trampling in the world,
in all the vineyards,
and all the wine pouring forth, cannot nourish

That one isolated spot
which is where you stand
with a dry throat

And shriveled heart.
You are the only immoral soul
on the ground when the gods have tripped you up.

Oh—Bring out the chorus.
What last Me of all the "*Me*'s" have there been
and had to be?

The snake sloughs off its skin
not to renew itself but only to survive.
Who is left to recite a prayer for the would-be dead?

III. Lord and Lady of Sustenance

In the highest of the thirteen heavens
they met in their teens.
It was nineteen forty-seven, a.d.

She got pregnant,
not in the backseat of a Studebaker,
on the sofa in the parlor,

Or in the obscurity of school grounds
long after the janitor had gone—
but on a lumpy sack of garlic heads

That they had picked by sundown,
and which felt like the hump of an alligator.
She would swear forever—

Forever being the next thirty-seven years—
that is what broke her back
and not *la pizca*—

The picking they did
season after season.
He was her cousin,

Once removed.
For Mexicans, that still made him her cousin.
The family was from Morelos.

Neither she nor he—Lord and Lady
of their medieval lives,
in the twentieth-century landscape of U.S. agriculture

Knew the wondrous Santa Patria first hand,
of which their parents spoke with such nostalgia.
The pair doubted its existence. Elsewise,

Why would their people have fled
like thieves,
traitors,

To go where they would be so despised?
Oh—
The newlyweds had hardly attended school,

Not like the contracts promised.
They were put to work right away,
earning half the pay of the adults.

Children, being smaller, tiring faster,
picked less. But
every cent counted.

The family of the new
Lord and Lady of Sustenance—
grew as it moved from shack to shack

Their children were not welcome in schools—
"Dirty Little Mexicans"
should be working in the sun.

Braceros were the manpower
brought in when gringos
were off fighting the war.

An agreement between
two governments
to use Mexican laborers as surplus.

The Lord and Lady never had much.
She, no wedding band,
nor he, a store-bought shirt.

But
they were
in love,

And long-suffering both.
Every day they complained.
They were not dignified or stoic,

At peace or even resigned
to their lot.
And why should they have been?

One died of a heart attack
shortly after the other—of diabetes complications—
long before any imagined retirement plan

For farm workers.
Ella did not bury them or show up at their funerals,
long gone—like a gazelle,

First chance she got—
she went running,
fast—

From the stories at sunset,
puros cuentos,
pollen in the air, enough to make you choke—

The stories of *Ometecutli*: Two Lord,
and his consort, *Omecihuatl*: Two Lady,
who took turns trying to make them/us forget:

The day in the fields,
the bushels we filled by quota,
calluses on our cracked little hands,

As if made of black Oaxacan clay
dried in the pitch of the day's heat.
Trying to make us forget

The sun that caused fevers,
blistered lips and feet,
made you see spots for years after,

Forget
the beans we had for supper again,
the last baby that died soon after birth,

The *tío* suffering of tuberculosis
when each morning he rose with the rest,
coughing, coughing.

Grandparents we never spent
a birthday with, whom we hardly knew
left back in Morelos—

Morelos,
otherwise known as Paradise
in the dreams and nightmares

Of all
when and if we got to sleep.
To forget

The contaminated water we washed in,
drank.
To forget parasites

Proliferating in our intestines,
to forget
our mother's moans which meant

Another baby soon coming,
to forget
forget

Forget
which was, always, oh—
so much better

Than remembering—
the shrewd trick
of Jews and Blacks in America,

And the descendants of whites colonized in Europe—
everyone seemed to know
they must remember

Or be lost—
obliterated
like a video game figure

Game over,
forever.
You're just another immigrant population,

Get in line.
Not true,
in this case.

The *mestizo* of Post-Conquest America,
part *indio*
and part Explorer Eurotrash

Forgets everything.
As did *she—Ella*
as did I

Try hard when *we* left,
ran off to Laredo,
only holding on to something—

Good,
small as it might be,
the size of a seed in the palm of

Ometecutli's hand,
remember Mother—the very real mother,
not of myth or legends,

Not a bigger than life Hayworth at the Saturday
matinee with *tía* Renata,
but a farmhand with white hair at thirty

And a tumor the size
of a cantaloupe in her belly that was never removed,
and made us think she was pregnant

Again,
and Father—
el padre de Ella—la Otra

Whose right eye was pulled out
by a wild branch
when he bent down

For the six hundredth and second time
that day
to yank a rich

Ripe
red
tomato

That would end up in the house salad
that came with the daily special
in a Saratoga diner.

When he got back from the hospital,
the rancher gave him a day off.
That was before lawsuits

Were the modus operandi in *los Estados*,
which didn't mean
a farmworker could sue

Even
for an
eye.

No.
Oh—
It goes without saying,

Without trying to be shocking,
suggestive, or heaven forbid,
self-pitying

Or—
or—
or—

May I add this:
sensationalist,
alarmist,

Or Communist.
Wait.
I forgot.

There are no communist threats left—
(except for Castro,
who only threatens his own now),

Replaced by fearless
terrorists—
ferret attack

Challenging
charging
elephants.

(Meanwhile, I remain painfully conscious
of avoiding the real subject which was
my dear and beloved parents.)

You can love your mother and father
even if
they put you to work at eleven.

Even if
there were no occasions for celebration.
Even if they never stood up to anybody in your defense.

Et cetera,
et cetera.
You love them for begetting you.

Yes,
like in the Old Testament,
to keep working other people's lands.

I held on to the little things,
stashed in crevices,
to pull out when I really needed them.

The time, for instance,
when my mother kept both of us in
to cure my chronic ear infection.

She warmed olive oil on the hot plate,
poured it in my ear with a borrowed dropper
and used a luxuriant piece

Of cotton from an aspirin bottle to keep it in.
I remember the aroma of her flour tortillas on the *comal*.
As for my father:

He leaned over and whispered,
"You look just like your mother—
the prettiest woman

I've ever known."
He kissed me on the brow.
That was how he said he loved me.

I was twelve.
He was thirty-three.
A Russian pianist told me once that we are obsessed

With age in America.
We are as young as we feel,
she said.

She was wrong.
When you work like that you get old fast.
You are never young,

No matter what you tell yourself
after twenty, thirty, forty—
you ache all over

But most especially
your heart:
reservoir

Of all misfortune
pertinent
to you.

You,
you,
yes, you.

My father said his parents told him,
"Now, you've done it,
marry the girl," and he did.

Or that's how they both told it.
There were no photo albums.
No one found evidence in that blue

Suitcase Mother carried from place to place—
like she was ever going
anywhere.

We were all baptized.
That was the extent of her religious convictions.
She didn't want her children to die and go straight to hell.

She had her ideas,
implacable.
Father was

Lord over nobody.
But we could not talk back.
We could not look him in the eye.

(Yes, the one eye he had left.)
We could not laugh too much
or too loud around him,

Or her.
They were, without doubt, made for each other,
like a trunk that got split by a ray of lightning,

With roots extending deep
down, beneath the earth, that entwine
and speak to each other in silence

Unable to extract,
no matter droughts or rains.
You could get as close to them

When they were working,
or eating, or resting or riding in the truck,
squeeze right between them and you still couldn't hear

What they were communicating to each other.
They didn't even move their lips.
But they were saying something.

One would nod,
the other shook his head. A decision
made. The fate of one of us to be announced

At the designated time. All we knew was that
the Double-Headed God above all the heavens,
above all the ordinary kind, declared together.

He, in plaid flannel shirt, frayed at the cuffs,
and faded bandana around his brow
and she, with the same cotton dress

Tía Delfina gave her when we worked with them
in Michigan.
And at night she slept in his socks.

She was cold-blooded, she said:
friolente.
It sounds different in Spanish—

It just means cold-blooded,
not implying amphibian origins,
or homicidal tendencies,

Necessarily.
Sometimes, we heard her giggling in the dark
after they thought we were asleep.

I always wondered and wonder still,
what—
was it that he said that made her laugh

Like a girl again,
in the dark,
on an old worn-out bed used by one migrant family

After the next,
with broken springs and mattress,
pissed on by diapered infants

And Mamá–
with a rough Army blanket pulled over her head,
in his socks, a ratty sweater,

Muffled laughter, mouth closed,
laughing nonetheless,
like she never did in the day

Like she never did with any of us,
laughing quietly
in the arms of her man.

IV. Mamá Grande

The First Mother,
Mother Before Time Began,
The Primordial Grandmother

The old woman had lived in the back
Of her eldest son's—*el Jefe*'s—house,
in two rooms made of wooden planks,

Not much more than a shack,
but neat and clean,
with a stone floor.

Outside were the toilet and cold shower.
There were two brother roosters
and a full chicken coop to peck your feet.

That was the best that *el Jefe*
could do for his mother
in her last years. She was—what—ninety

When she died?
Great-grandmother,
with a head of pearl-white spun silk

And every day she wore an apron,
the mark of one
who does her own chores.

The great-granddaughter noted all this
early on during family visits,
rest stops, as it were,

Between harvests to pick.
A vacation of sorts,
in a place where a private shower and outhouse

Without flies were luxuries,
despite the eternal stillness and dessicating heat
of the *canícula* afternoons.

As if on Pluto—
whether gas giant or escaped moon—
heavy

Hours elongated into black holes,
interrupted only
by daily deliveries

Of the ice man,
tortilla man,
fruit vendor,

The lady who offered home permanents,
mail, now and then:
ads for a movie-star magazine,

A record club,
the electric bill, news from a far-off
relative.

Ella se puso a grabar cada detalle
like a lithograph,
a detective for future mapping.

She started with Mamá Grande's soft hands,
like crushed orchids,
pale and brown-spotted.

Then came the under-slip
(still put away in a trunk),
that Mamá Grande had made of a pink cotton remnant

And crocheted embroidery along the hem
for the great-granddaughter,
the summer when she was ten.

(*Or had she been twelve?*
No—
At eleven she'd begun to bleed.

After that, she herself was put to stitch.
She no longer played with the children.
And her mother—her very real mother—

Of the Burnt Sienna color without oil mixed,
Raw Umber and some odd shade of blue
kept her in,

To roll out dough, boil beans,
learn to make rice
and to iron shirts right.)

Mamá Grande, too,
had an iron-tight recall
of everything that happened in her youth,

Within the hundred mile or so radius
where she had spent her life.
She especially recounted the *Revolución*,

The famous train ride with Pancho Villa
to Torreón.
(Which was the highlight of all the downtrodden

Born before nineteen-ten,
whether they had been there or not.)
Once Mamá Grande pulled

Her great-granddaughter aside with the yank
and lack of tenderness reserved for pre-adolescents
who must be civilized.

She sat her on the floor between her knees,
and started to check for lice,
a ritual that often came

With warnings and complaints
And what was then
incomprehensible advice.

Cipactli shouted from the galaxies.
The Earth Monster
whose eyes made springs

And mouth, the rivers and caverns,
her nose, the valleys,
and hair, the trees and tall grasses.

Mamá Grande was grand,
all right.
Tho' the child could not have yet said why.

She just knew to sit quietly
and not let anything get by,
not an utterance under breath,

A scolding undeserved,
the slightest observance.
It was her instinct forming, perhaps.

"Don't think, *muchacha*," the Earth Monster began,
"that I was ever one of those women
who followed so-called soldiers

"Like a mule
with a stone *metate* on my back
to grind the corn for their meals,

"Forced to lay with whatever pig
claimed me. *¡Qué asco!*
Not me.

"When the *Federales* came and ransacked
our homestead,
I hid

"Up in a tree.
Yes I did.
In the night I ran away.

"I lived in the desert
and ate grubs and cactus
of every shape and variety.

"I followed *los zopilotes* circling above
(maybe they were following me—
all skin and bones that I was!)

"And whenever they were done
feeding off some carrion
They led me to water to drink.

"One day
I wandered upon a village where a girl told me:
'You're pretty, *güeno*, not half bad anyway.'

"I made my living in a saloon after that.
We danced with the *Federales*,
Los Carranzistas, Villistas, Colorados.

"We danced with *Zapatistas*,
Ay, you know, *hija?*
It didn't matter.

"Men were men
even then.
We danced and we drank and yes,

"We took their money.
It was all the same.
And in paper, mostly worthless anyway.

"When the *Revolución* was over,
it was time to go home,
each his or her own way.

"My family never knew.
They thought I had been kidnapped.
But my father was very angry

"And more bitter with our losses.
We were the big shots of our region.
We were white and with all the pedigree

"You want.
He would have put up a reward for his best horse,
but not for me.

"'It takes one night out for milk to spoil,'
my father declared. It didn't matter
whose fault it had been.

"It didn't matter what had happened,
not just to a girl
but to a whole country.

"'What?' I said, one day,
up to here with him.
'You think no one will have me?'

"'*Adiós*,' I said, 'good riddens,'
and went right out the door.
I took up with the *indio* who

"branded the animals.
My father ran us off.
He called me a whore.

"That *indio* became my husband for the next
forty-four years.
He was…

"*Comme ci comme ça.*"
That's French," she said with a knuckle-rap
on the girl's head when she looked up.

"As a husband a little mean,
particularly when drunk on *pulque*.
It was what *patrones* gave them

"As pay for their work.
A revolution fought for *pulque*
and everything else, the same.

"But what could one do?
In my day
a woman needed protection from a man—

"To protect her from other men.
If my father had just left me
a little land, *un cachito.*

"I could have gone back.
I could have planted *maíz*, some beans.
I'd have fed my children.

"I had no use for men.
They held no surprise.
After the first few you see the pattern.

"Yes, you will hear one day
women say all men are the same.
That's because they are.

"But my father wouldn't accept me,
ungrateful as he said I was.
My mother had nothing to say about it.

"And tho' we all fought the revolution
to have a little land,
to plant a little food,

"Just to make ends meet.
What they were really talking about
was that it would be for some men

"To own, to decide, to order the women and children
and donkeys and whipped oxen.
And of course, other men, too."

Sometimes such stories are
shared in kitchens or imparted
on starlit porches.

Other times a woman
talks as she is combing her
great-granddaughter's hair,

Meticulously, evenly, slowly.
"It's okay," Mamá Grande said on that occasion,
as she tied a bright red ribbon entwined

In the rope of virgin hair hanging,
a *mecate* down the back
of the young girl

In pink slip where beneath
nipples like raisins
visible only to the barefaced stare.

"*Está bien*—if you share property with a man,
buy a plot of land, the materials for a house,
build it together.

"Just know the law
and know what is yours.
Know your worth."

Then, without having asked,
made an announcement,
requested the father's permission,

Or even wondered if the girl would have consented,
Mamá Grande cut the braid with her
sewing scissors.

With a sharp *zas*,
unrecoverable and no way to retract,
gone just like that.

"Here," Mamá Grande said,
handing over the severed tresses,
"One day you'll need a few pesos.

"You can sell this.
When all accounts are made,
you will always be your most reliable resource."

V. *Cipactli*: Woman as Monster

Subterranean behemoth
never had a beginning,
a cyclonic humpback

Thrashing about
in the ocean
of chaos.

I am she,
y Ella será siempre
before.

The child's head appeared,
then its tiny body,
then its scream.

I am a colossal toad with mouths
at all my joints,
dripping blood.

I am a shark,
a sawfish,
a leviathan dragon to rival all

Who the god of the morning
and the god of night,
coiled in the form of serpents

Pull apart.
Jealous each
to lord over me.

Soy Ella–la Otra
who once was
whole.

Now I am She
and I have always been
me,

Unnatural, as it seems,
from before
the beginning.

VI. Left-handed Brother

She was thirteen and he twenty-one
when he enlisted.
Twenty years into his career

He would fly over Kuwait
and never be seen again:
"A hero," the letter to the family read.

She liked him when she was a girl
because he talked to her,
unlike anyone else around,

Unlike their mother,
unlike their father,
the other siblings,

And various migrant teachers
they had from school
to school.

To his death he went
with a royal entourage,
carrying a red flute broken in half.

Lord and warrior
brandished both sword and staff.
He was not a god but the symbol of one,

In the manner which the true lords of the land
dealt with their young soldiers at war
in order to sacrifice them.

In the end, the brother turned warrior
Had no wife, no home but three
Girlfriends to whom he wrote from time to time.

Their letters neatly collected in his sack.
And then there was this:
A four for a quarter,
black and white from a dime-store machine.

Picture of his baby sister—*Ella*,
taken during the unspoken days
in Tamoanchan.

Flower Feather
Precious Flower
"Your privates are like that

Of a rose bud," her mother once told her.
The closest they ever got
to Sex Education.

From the vulva of Xochiquetzal
came the flowers in Paradise.
And from that part of the vulva stolen

from the sleeping goddess
taken to the Underworld—
came the most wondrous of scents.

Left-handed brother who never loved her
who forced her to the cabana
where he was sure

No one would find them
carried her kicking,
pounding his chest,

Pinching his cheeks.
Cut it out.
cut it out.

It's not funny anymore.
He would not accept that
she did not want him

Until the dogs came
barking,
came barking,

And snapped him
out of his dream,
his self-delusion.

After all, he had said to himself:
Look how she looked at him
when they worked in the sun.

Surely that was longing
in those dark eyes in the fields.
Oh, yes.

How she wanted him
or else—what about how much
she sought him out,

To talk of things,
pretended what she wanted
was to talk...?

He left for the Army.
She ran away. They saw
each other only at family reunions

That was, when she came around.
All the while—forever after—
until the night his aircraft blew up

A meteorite in the sky,
nothing but a flashing light
for a second or two

Until it vanished
as if it never was,
as if he had arrived

At the last of the Nine Hells
of Mictlan and the reward
was annihilation of the soul—

the left-handed brother, demise of her innocence,
remained convinced she had wanted him
that summer long ago.

VII. *La Tía* Renata

The July she ran away
before the end of cotton season,
it was Aunt Renata who took her in.

La tía Renata, of the whitest of skin
and the blackest hair swept back
in a horse's tail

That swung with every swish of full hips;
a widow's peak resting like an eagle's beak
on her crown. *Tía* Renata was not an aunt by blood

But by marriage and circumstance.
A nurse—*el Jefe* only allowed her
to practice at home.

The poor came for an injection,
a salve,
a mending of bones.

The son was sent to military school,
the daughter, to the nuns.
Surrounded by biting red ants, crawling cactus,

At night the yelping coyotes,
except for the occasional patient,
tía Renata's existence was rendered to silence.

A fuchsia sun froze in the sky in midday.
Wild *urracas* laughed in the distance.
Everything stayed away

Until he died.
And when he did, *Ella* came,
tho' she couldn't say why.

"You'll sleep next to me," Renata told
the run-away niece with calloused hands
and all that she held in her name:

A pair of men's jeans,
a pint of whiskey and a dry
tube of mascara. The aunt lay in bed

One toe pointed to the other knee,
like a tired ballerina or the Tarot Hangman
that meant there were still things to figure out.

In the dark, *tía* Renata—who reigned over silence now—
whispered, "I used to help women be free.
Come," she said louder, and together they went to see.

Far up on the highest shelf in the pantry
mason jars beyond anyone's eye or reach.
Aunt Renata pointed the flashlight at each.

She was called *la doctora*, *la santa*, and to others:
Angel of their salvation.
Lined up, floating inside,

Neither grinning or with grimace,
but faceless, in fact, preserved for what purpose—
Ella couldn't guess.

"Look," *tía* Renata said,
"and remember this:
To hurt a child is a sin.

"Send the soul back to God if you can't love it.
The unborn become *tlaloques*
and join the clouds to give us rain.

They play in the mountains of
Tamoanchan
until they are called here again.

"Oh"—sighed *tía* Renata of the impossible hair
and the impossible skin, as she fell to the floor.
"Oh," I sighed, too, in her hand-stitched gown,

The first I had ever worn,
the first I had ever owned,
was in that desert home long ago.

VIII.   Dog Days of Summer '75

In the dog days
of that summer
they drove to Chicago

In *tía* Renata's
'63 Buick.
It had been *el Jefe*'s

And the aunt had just learned
to drive.
It was a harrowing ride

To say the least,
but worth it
once they arrived

In a city that glimmered
like emeralds,
shone like glass.

"We'll take a room,"
The widowed aunt said, who
by the minute revealed that her recklessness

Was not confined to the way
she drove.
No.

That summer when the niece
was eighteen
and she left *los files*

(In other words,
working in the fields
from Harlingen to Oregon,

Following one harvest
after the next),
Renata in a new wardrobe:

Off the shoulder
Ava Gardner frocks
and open-toed slip-ons

Taught the girl
how to drive on the Texas road.
By the time they reached Indiana

She preferred the wheel
and let the aunt sleep off
the beer she drank alone.

It was clear the adventure
had everything to do
with letting loose

Away from eyes
and tongues of
neighbors and pious churchgoers,

And nothing to do
with whether *la tía* Renata
was ever out of touch

With her true inclinations
that apparently had only needed the right
environment in order

To manifest,
not like
an experiment in a petri dish.

But more like an unearthed
tyrannosaurus egg
ready to hatch.

The niece was eighteen
that summer
and she would never be again.

She was also a virgin—
Except for the
petting with her brother

That took place in the dark
while the rest of the family
slept the sleep of the half-dead

All in the same room,
or the last time when the brother
and sister snuck off

To check out the wealthy grower's pool area
and nearly did it
in one of the cabanas

But the watch-dogs came
barking,
came barking.

And while they hid
until it was safe to leave
they cooled off

And cooled down.
He blamed her and
she blamed him

For the trouble they would be in
back at work,
where each bushel they picked

Counted,
and each hand
counted

And their father had not had
so many children
to have the hands

Doing things such as they
two had done
in the dark.

Aside from the family stuff
that at the time
she thought was part of growing up,

She was about as naïve
as a girl in those times
could be.

Not after *tía* Renata
that summer
when she said,

"Let's pick up a couple
of men. Have you ever done
that? It's easy.

All men are easy."
And that is what they did.
Once

Tía Renata emptied out the wallet
of one *tonto* who left it on the table
when he went to the toilet.

She didn't need the money.
She had all of *el Jefe*'s life insurance.
She did it out of contempt

For the gringo stockbroker
who said his wife
from Winnetka

Was away with the kids
visiting her parents
and he was looking for some

Hot Spanish girls like they were.
"Come lick my pussy," she heard
her aunt whisper in a thick accent

That sounded like La Lupe
who was the talent in the raw
singer with Tito Puente

When Viet Nam reels every
night on TV News,
the Bay of Pigs stand-off,

Assassination of a Catholic
Irish president,
and a generation around the world

in mass protest against
a symphony of dictators
conducted by Kissinger

Set the stage for the horrors
of globalization—
the horror of one man

Always being the profit of
another—
and then Renata's tongue wet his ear.

"I'll be right back," the *tonto*
slurred and before he did,
they ran. They tumbled into the street

Laughing,
Laughing,
howling

Until the bouncer came out
and said "Get lost.
This ain't that kind of place."

So many things she learned
with her aunt those days.
Not just about men

And how to change a tire,
but about DNA
and RNA

And the stars,
and undiscovered planets,
and when you sang *La Malageña*

To make the falsetto break
or else don't sing it at all.
And what else she learned

Was not to cry
over anything
ever,

That there was never loss
only lessons
to be gained.

And for the sake of preventing
some mistakes,
a lot of unorthodox counseling.

When Aunt Renata said
it was time to go back
and she would not take her along,

She was not allowed to argue.
But just told to take the cash
to pay for one more week at the motel

While she started working "under-the-table"
washing dishes
at a posh restaurant downtown.

"There's nothing for you
back there,"
the aunt said with a kiss

On the mouth.
"Just don't
marry a *mariachi*—

You'll live the lonely life
of the doctor's wife
except with a drunk

Who spends all his money
before he gets home."
She left her the Buick

Which broke down a month later
and took a plane,
something

She had never done before.
The niece never knew
where that *loca* aunt had ended.

That was when long-distance calls
seemed such an extravagance
and no one wrote letters,

Or at least the aunt did not
answer any. The years passed
And *la tía* Renata had disappeared

Like Kaumari,
the Hindu Goddess:
a Cosmic Mother of Evil Intent

Who alternatively
lacks envy,
delusion.

Renata: *Reina de la frontera*
Border woman on every fringe
Peacock with male plumage

An arrow, an ax,
a bell, a book, a bow,
a cockerel,

A lotus flower
that grows
out of the mud,

A spear-like memory dug
deep in the back of a barracuda
off a Bahamian island

While an Argentine eccentric
camouflaged by foliage
sat in a dingy

Spying as *la tía* Renata waited
for the next boat
to the main island.

He spied on her fallen breasts,
and judged her aging hands
as she smoked

His forgotten cigarettes,
as if she were in her own
private garden

With nothing to do
and nowhere to go,
as if he hadn't sent her away

Out of cowardice
to face
his own varicose veins,

Cirrhotic liver,
erectile dysfunction
and assorted personality disorders,

All subdued by the pills
in the clutter of plastic vials
in his Gaugin-style thatch-roofed hut

That island girls
excused
for the nights of free-flowing rum

And because he claimed
he was famous someplace
where he got

A regular check
and bought them perfume
and Frank Sinatra records souvenirs,

So they'd dance bare-breasted
beneath the moonlight
on the shore when he fried mackerel

Over an open fire
until he passed out.
And they went home

Laughing
like the wind
through rustling palms.

Oh–
But our ol' gal didn't die then,
Not that year

Or the year after,
left in the hollow
of a coconut

Everything around white,
protected by a shell as hard and fibrous
as the Argentine's *cojones*.

Meanwhile, back in Chicago,
the niece left with one small bag
and a pair of the crazy aunt's earrings

Inside the motel room with matching drapes
and bedspread spotted with cigarette burns
and ominously stained sheets

And a print over the headboard
of a cove
and tropical fish

And a sun like a dot
of blood,
or taking a closer look

Which one night she did,
maybe it was
blood

Considering there were two more
dots like it
on the wall right next to the frame.

Then there were the nightly fake moans
in Room 817,
which was the one adjacent

To hers,
that belonged to Charmaine
who was really Mirta,

The Puerto Rican girlfriend
of the manager
and who in the day

Worked the streets
faking moans in cars.
"If he ever hits me," Mirta told

Her, "Call the police."
She stayed awake just to listen
after reruns of *Baretta*,

Playing *tía* Renata's transistor
and trying to copy
the tropical fish

On stationery she borrowed
from the reception desk
when the manager

Was busy banging
her friend.
Tiny fish with wings

With eyes on their tails,
with fins that sailed
across the sky.

When the blood sun dot
wasn't looking.
she *salsa*ed to the *Fania All Stars*

The condiment becoming a verb
when it meant
practicing the steps

Mirta taught her.
When the manager found
she soaked the linen in bleach

In the tub she became
Head of Housekeeping,
which meant

She got to clean all the sheets
which helped her save enough
to one day move out.

IX. *Renacimiento* (or, Death to All Dwarf Roosters Who Think They Can Fly)

You can forget everything
about your life
when you ride the train.

It goes underground,
then comes up into the light.
You watch what used to be

Back porches, laundry lines,
defunct refrigerators, junk stashed and piled high
and are now still back porches

But disguised as furnished decks
complete with barbecue pits
and flower boxes with geraniums.

But back then when she went from
job to her studio
she mostly rode with eyes closed.

They say it takes a mentor,
someone who can guide an
otherwise lost young woman

Like she was, to help realize
potential, ambition,
gain confidence.

In her case, it was a sign
on the train:
Community College: *Window*

To the World.
She registered for a couple
of night classes the next semester.

Biology 101 and an
art history course: from
Medieval to the Renaissance.

She had no idea when in history
those periods were,
only that they had to have been

Far enough from her own
to let her believe
that she might have then belonged,

Unlike the present
where she did not
belong anywhere.

She was alien,
not because she had antennae
or lacked a green card.

But because of what went on
in her head
and outside her head.

There was a white world
and there was a black world.
She fell through the cracks of the city's reality

In the Seventies.
What a shock, therefore,
when her biology teacher,

Her first professor
ever,
was brown.

They say—now—
that color doesn't matter,
that it's wrong to notice.

But not then
and then
was not

That long ago.
She had so rarely seen anyone
that looked

Like someone in her family
since she left *los files*
that she immediately

Felt
she could trust him,
tell him how she felt

Invisible and inconsequential.
When a stranger addressed her
she spoke with a very small voice

That was strangely accented
since she knew English fluently.
The psychology of feeling alien

Had made her mimic one,
maybe to make gringos
feel better when they believed

She was—had to be—a foreigner,
looking neither White nor Black,
which was how "American" was defined.

Those were the race dynamics
everywhere back then.
Back then

And now.
Back then and now.
(Except that now

There is an unprecedented number
of mixed-bloods
populating a new society.

That should help
democracy along
a tad.)

But getting back to the teacher—
not so young
and not old,

But at that stage
in a man's life
where he can't believe

He's slowing down,
was a brown man
with a Zapata moustache.

He laughed
like her *tío* Manuel
and was not embarrassed to tell the class

That he had had too much *chile*
for lunch when he had gas.
Gas being a natural part of being organic,

He added. He also had volunteered
with the United Farm Workers, knew
César Chávez personally, he said.

Yes,
she felt
she could trust him.

She looked forward to Tuesday nights.
She didn't dress up for him.
In those days everyone wore tattered jeans,

Even the professors.
But he was still impressive,
as the first educated brown man she'd ever met.

And if he could get there,
if he could learn so much,
if he could—so could she.

In class she looked at him as if she were mesmerized—
except when taking notes. She was, after all,
now a coed.

Although she'd never been on
a real campus or understood
about degrees

Or at that time, even realized
about the glass ceiling for a brown girl
such as she in any university.

But there she was
feeling the dream
the way only the young can dream,

The way Martin had felt it,
because he felt for everybody.
And who could take that from her

Watching her brown college professor
whose very presence seemed to say
anything was possible.

But she caught him looking not
at her eyes as she listened so
proudly to a man who could have

Been her uncle but was so confident
in front of Whites,
who showed not one iota

Of the humility she had seen
in her father and uncles with the ranch growers.
No.

He stared not at her eyes,
that her lovers would say later,
when she'd have them,

Had the depth of caves.
Tho' perhaps they had seen mystery
when in fact

She was tired
from boiling linen.
Sometimes,

She looked intense
when she was bored and trying hard
to call it an early night.

For whatever reason she had
that gaze that
passed for intriguing

And men found inviting,
her brown biology teacher
did not pretend

He cared much
what she thought.
She saw him stare

Through most of the lecture
on the evolution of the homo sapien
At her very womanly breasts.

Classes were held in a high school
which gave an atmosphere
of being in high school

When a bell clanged to signal
change of classes.
Once,

They even had a fire drill
which was a false alarm.
Some pranksters

Just like in high school,
only, of course,
it had been adult men.

Still, she liked the idea of being
in college.
She was in college,

She'd say to herself every day
and when she had plunked down her cash
for the used books

And when she said she had to stay in
to study for a test,
She felt like the moving train

That she took every day and every evening
and on Tuesdays got a transfer
for the bus to the high school that

At night
the city had turned into what
would be her alma mater.

Life should not always be so sad,
demasiado triste,
was something else she also told herself,

When she accepted a pizza date
with one of her classmates.
The subject of the biology teacher's eyes

Never came up.
Why should it?
Men stared.

(And let's remember,
This was way before sexual harassment laws
and stalking laws

And justice for rape or use of DNA for evidence.
If you even vaguely knew a man
your grocery delivery boy, let's say,

Or telephone man putting in a new outlet,
the fact that you had let him in
was as good as consent to sex.

Well,
You know what comes next.
But it's not as bad as you think.)

She fought the biology teacher—
Brown and familiar like her *tío*,
But daunted by his book sense,

Until he got hold of her in the hall,
wrestled her to the ground.
Still, she dug nails

Into his forearms
as he tried to get a leg in between
her own. Then the bell rang.

The bell rang.
Students would be out any minute.
Someone would see them.

Someone would call for help.
They would see
what the biology teacher

Was really about—
not smart at all,
but stupid.

Stupid.
Más tonto que la jodida.
They would see even if

There were no laws then
to help guard
the virgins of the village,

Someone,
maybe another young woman
like herself

Would see them struggling
on the floor and horrified
that it could have been her,

She'd scream.
No one came.
As if time had frozen all around them,

No one came.
She felt his blistering breath.
She felt his spit.

"A man," he whispered,
"will pursue a woman
for ten years,

If it takes that long to make
her his own.
Just to make her his, that's all."

Then they both heard a click,
a door opening. He helped her up,
like a gentleman, a real *caballero*.

She allowed him to do so.
(What a kick,
she thought years later.)

Just before he straightened
his thinning hair and then his collar.
He laughed a little nervous

Laugh under this breath,
walking off like he owned the world,
or at least a small piece of it.

We never went back—
Not *Ella*/I—
to Biology 101.

As for Medieval
and Renaissance Art History
I memorized about two hundred

Slides, maybe a thousand altogether.
It was, after all,
some time ago.

The white woman instructor
never said two words to *us*—
Not to her and not to me—

The only comment on the exams,
in an almost illegible hand:
You should learn to spell before

Taking a college course
such as mine,
Despite our earning

One hundred percent correct
on all exams,
dates, artists, titles,

The important facts of each piece.
While I took notes
during lectures

Ella—la Otra—
sketched
dwarf roosters who wanted to fly

In wide checkered ties
with hard-ons
falling from balloons sailing

Across a Florentine sky,
dropping inside laboratory
beakers boiling with acid.

Oh—cruel was their death,
Yet curiously amusing.
It was not the kind of acid

That dissolved the flesh
but the kind that sent imagination swirling—
dissolved only the staring

Of the aero-inept fowl in LSD baths.
All this delight
from a cheap fountain pen

And a graphed notebook.
And to think, she (and I) had yet
to discover Hieronymus Bosch.

X. The Sire

As Osiris
opposed Ra
in ancient Egypt,

and the Quetzal Snake
in America
turned from the Sun God

And rose
as the Morning Star,
as Buddha left wealth behind him,

The man who would be
The sire had once also
Wanted nothing more

Than to fight dragons in the name
of Something Huge and Indisputable.
But didn't find it.

He dropped out of college
where he had majored in philosophy
for six years.

The would-be Sire then began
to write lyrics for a band,
spurred by what he was certain then

The Voice of his Calling.
But what that calling was
when his girlfriend told him

She was pregnant
he hadn't yet heard.
The new father

Went to work as a
machine operator
with an uncle back

In the East Bay, California,
where his single mother
had raised him.

He sent for his young wife
and their child.
For a while they were a family.

They did what modest families
did. They ate meals
together.

They slept
together.
They enjoyed each other's

Conversations.
But he never stopped asking
himself

Who he was,
apart from what
was expected of him.

And why was she there.
The obvious answers came.
His own mother

Pointed them out
when he'd confide
his confusion,

Which he often did.
He was there
as a man.

It was his duty.
A man did not
abandon

His children
or a good wife,
which,

Until she left him—
she seemed to be.
And when she did,

Again, his mother,
who had raised him
without a father,

Reminded him of his duty.
And tho' he did not seek
his mother's approval

As his wife always accused,
he did make the effort not
to displease her.

His uncle
reminded him to be strong.
His friends assured him

That there were plenty of skirts around,
better
prettier,

More worthy than she,
Not to mention
not *as* perverse.

(The mention of her perversion
made his mother lose all
sympathy for her),

She—
with her strange imagistic paintings which
he had encouraged.

He pampered her. He was compassionate
when she menstruated,
Folded into an accordion with cramps

As for her odd new acquaintances
with whom she stayed out late—
he said nothing,

Like a reasonable man
who understood a wife
should not always be at home.

When they were short on money
he worked on weekends
and took a second job.

Dutiful husband that he was
who would not ever show
he worried fitfully over

The chance he might somehow fail
in protecting her,
caring for her,

Loving her
enough.
He never cheated. He did not drink.

Tho' who would have blamed him,
when after the baby
she lost interest.

The Stripper Clubs were just
a way to get a release.
Nothing like

Her betrayal.
Where had God gone
in those dark days following the night

He found the two women
sleeping in his bed?
Long gone, too

Was his passion for music,
the Led Zeppelin dreams of his youth,
and all that were suddenly left

Was this stranger
of a woman
in his home

And the beautiful child
that she would
no doubt

Corrupt.
And tho' he loved the boy,
Inasmuch as her blood

Ran in his veins, too,
and those were her eyes
that looked back

(Tho' the rest of the face was his),
he found it hard
to call the boy his own.

It was war
in court.
Each fought with acrimony

He almost
won
custody.

When he didn't,
he quit
his job.

He took up the guitar again
and with not the first or the second
or even the third

Woman he lived with
after that,
he settled down

To such an uninspired
life of normality
that when he had a

Stroke,
it actually
excited him.

XI. *La Amazona* (or, The Eighties in San Francisco)

Daughter of Ares—
Greek god of War—
her name means

Compelling Men
to Mourn:
Penthesilea.

Amazonian queen,
goddess or myth.
Why don't we throw

A party for her?
Call a national holiday?
The Mediterranean,

Aegean and Black Seas,
even the Bosphorus
never knew one again

Such as She.
Like Sappho,
her victories are long

Annihilated.
Without evidence
there is no history.

But we could invent
her story,
we could make us she,

Rodrigo Reyes and I thought
it a good idea as we planned
a costume ball for the artists.

He and I were a team.
Oh—*él fue hermano de Ella*
and my partner in crime,

He, with his resonant voice,
silver-streaked hair at fifty,
and among the few I've known

This side of Mexico City
who knew how to *danzón*.
The first of my friends who yielded

With more agony than grace
when AIDS arrived,
pounding hatefully

Without mercy
like Ares, whose chariot
was pulled by Terror and Fear.

La Amazona,
he named me—
as an endearment,

Of course,
con cariño.
He adored

The masculine
in a woman,
the feminine

In men.
We are all
one of each.

Or at least
that's what he said.
He made a pertinent

Inquiry once.
It became a challenge.
"Why,"

He asked on a rare clear
day in San Francisco,
"are you married?

"Think of five good reasons.
Okay,
give me one."

Rodrigo Reyes was my twin.
He could ask me such things
and not have an eye pulled,

Thumbs cut off.
He himself had no husband,
no need for men

Aside from sex.
Except
for the runaway,

A scarred Narcissus,
with needle-tracked skin,
who robbed him

And was found later
seared
like a salmon,

From liver to throat,
stinking up the restroom
of the cross-dresser bar

Where Rodrigo Reyes
emceed in tux
and patent leather shoes.

The authorities suspected
him
but the slain lover was an illegal

A junky to boot.
Nothing was done
and we went on

For a time like that,
feeling free,
which is all you can do

When you talk about
freedom,
is to feel it.

He got sick.
The carousing continued.
Why not?

That's what he lived for.
That's how he died.
After one last carnival

In Veracruz. But before then
he carried my pouch
of sharpened arrows.

My cauterized breast
did not repulse him.
He counted

On my aim.
He especially enjoyed
my horsemanship.

Something to see on the hills
of San Francisco.
This was right after Haight Ashbury

And before the Great Digital Divide—
when Berkeley still belonged to the Socialists
and San Jose was a sleepy Mexican town.

When cafes had names like Figaro's and Artemis
and bookstores were owned by booklovers
who read everything they sold

And when a poet walked in
you'd think it was Elvis *Live*.
So there I was, a young mother

With my child flung over the
left hip, the bow over the right
shoulder because

You'd never know.
Amazons were always on call.
To begin with

You had to slay three enemy men
before anyone gave you
any credit.

Yeah.
Amazons only fought men then.
There were only men then—

Fighting on the other side.
That's what made the Amazons
Amazons.

I didn't even battle against the woman
who picked up my man
(the moment I left him.)

He was duly maimed.
His joints dislocated as a baby
by his mother,

Another *Amazona.*
He was hardly doing me any good.
Rodrigo Reyes was right.

Lose the dead weight
if you're going to fight.
It's in the manual

For women warriors,
page 587,
third paragraph down.

I got around not having to
break my own son's limbs
due to a precedent

I found
in the Machu Picchu version
of Amazonian legacy.

The Great Incas might
have won had they taken
the women

Into knighthood
And not as their mistresses.
You have to admit

I had a point.
Boys, therefore, raised
by Amazons,

Tho' we were
a selected but brave
resurrected breed,

Were bound
to know that a woman
was not to be fooled with.

Fast forward fifteen years
here I am wondering,
(tho' ever so quietly to myself),

Old gal or old guard,
I won't say it out loud—
the young ones are busy

Celebrating
their privilege to choose
gender long after they were born.

Some feel they don't even need
an operation.
It's enough to say it.

It rendered the need for Amazons ineffective,
whose primary objective was
(if he might remember)

To defend women's rights.
Even women who chose to act
like men

And dress like men,
and did the kinds of work
men did

And called themselves men
were still women.
Not anymore.

So, I wonder, like I've said,
a thought that filters through,
plenty of miscellaneous

And extraneous information
no one seems to have much use for
anymore,

To the extent that
a person is forced to doubt
the purpose of experience,

Yet, wondering I am,
if it is just possible
that we, with all our sincerity,

Our zest for argument,
shrewd documentation,
finesse

For the art of persuasion,
picket lines,
petitions for changing policies,

Our birthright to breastfeed
when and where necessary
were wrong.

And no matter what we did,
Mamá Grande was right
about the Y chromosome.

XII. Governess of the Subconscious

She stopped traffic.
No,
she really did.

That was before
she made sergeant,
and later,

Chose to work
undercover
"Like

Serpico,"
she'd tease, knowing
my thing

For Pacino,
although she had preferred
him

In *Cruising*,
which went without saying
why.

We met in a bar.
Where else then, would you have known
who you were talking to was safe

To talk to
that way?
She was a cop,

Okay,
but she wasn't
a stereotype,

A bulldyke,
una *marimacha*,
manflor, butch.

At least
not on the outside.
There were plenty of those

Identifiers
in the bar
when I first dropped in on one.

How it happened was almost by
accident.
Although we know

There are no accidents,
only the gods giving
puppet shows

For their personal
amusement.
They chose *her* that time

To perform—
(*Ella, la Otra*—
the other side of me.

I'm not
schizoid.
Don't worry.

I
don't hear
voices

Like my ex-husband.
No question,
she is me

Concentrated.)
She/I/we
were chosen

To walk in that bar
in answer to
an ad

To wait tables.
"No experience
necessary."

(We got a good laugh
out of that
later)

She checked IDs at the door.
You always get your IDs checked
in gay bars.

Even if you're
decrepit,
they ask you to show them

And mean it,
since a slip could end with
a fast closing down.

"Let me see
an ID,"
that's what she did to me

When I first walked in.
I thought it was about giving me
a hard time.

"I have to support myself,"
I said, "I'm desperate,"
I added, like she needed to know.

"So?" She smiled,
"What Latina in this town isn't?"
She eventually let me pass up

Her bouncer's banter to
talk to the manager.
The next night after work

She invited me out.
Just
like that.

"Okay," I answered.
That's how I got
my membership card,

Fully initiated,
paid my dues right up, too,
When she left me

For the new waitress
right before
my very eyes.

Did not even apologize.
The manager clued me in.
"Next time,

Don't give it up so fast,"
Wow.
What an epiphany,

A virtual moment
of major proportions:
to discover that

Not only men
were
assholes.

Oh—believe it.
Once, my cop girl
caught me crying

In the bathroom.
No one had seen me cry.
Not since my aunt

Slapped me
when
holding back tears,

The day she got into a cab
then vanished.
I wouldn't cry when my parents died

Six months apart.
One anxious
to join the other.

That was true love.
Or the end of two difficult lives.
I didn't cry

When I'd given birth
without
so much as an Aspirin.

But I cried then,
in public.
"You'll get over me," she said.

I didn't want to be over her.
Moreover, I didn't want her
over me.

Just then the new waitress walked in.
Next thing
fists were flying, landing hard.

Someone ended up
with three stitches above her lip.
And it wasn't me.

I did not
get over her.
I hung on

Like Jonah with the whale, hung on
like to a truth,
as if it were real.

I
refused
to forget

The two weeks we spent,
silly, little incidents,
reading the Sunday paper together

The video we watched on the couch,
and then this:
how she reached over and down,

And my heart began to pound
like a girl's with a crush
in a parked Camaro

And I pulled back while
she pulled me in.
I heard my mother's warnings.

I saw the outline of a Sister of Mercy
her broad-winged wimple hovering over me.
I held my breath,

But my heart was pounding
like a symphony drum,
BOM BOM BOM

So loud the neighbors upstairs
surely heard it
not to mention, all the other sounds

We made.
A Plutonic mating in reverse.
Not like animals in the forest.

Not like wild cats or gentle fawn.
Not winged or skittering,
whipping about in a den.

We did not howl or screech.
We did not become multi-headed creatures,
multi-armed or multi-tongued.

We killed no one in our insatiable quest
for each other,
Swallowed no one whole.

We did not become monsters.
And the fact of my motherhood
and her choice not to bear,

Had brought to the other
no power nor caused the other fear.
I could be accused

Of my attraction in the mirror
and such conceits. I don't know what she
thought when she saw that

I loved her,
the word of all the words
bandied throughout the world

That should never
ever
be spoken

Without a test of fire.
Everything in the universe from
as far away as boiling red Mars

Forbade me her.
There was no returning.
There would be no forgiveness.

The jealous gods would incarnate.
They would hide behind rocks
waiting to tempt me

I would be beheaded,
die a million deaths,
each more dreadful than the last.

No one like men with clout
develop such a taste for Sadism.
I would be sent

To the Land of the Dead
without a dog to guide me,
without a basket of bread,

Without a single servant in attendance.
I would die like a dog
without a burial,

Without mourners or prayers in my name.
The scavengers would eat my eyes out.
My kin would say they never knew me.

And yet, that woman of mine
pulled
me in.

And I did not resist,
far from it.
Chalchiuhtlicue—

Water Goddess,
Patroness of the Sea,
Governess of the Subconscious,

Ever flowing
Liquid Sky,
reached over and down,

And pulled by the undertow,
a gush,
never seen or heard before

A sudden rushing cascade
of sheer salacity,
lust unleashed before me

Cushions drenched
when women spent, limbs entwined,
for what I believed then would be eternity.

Oh–
Believe it.
Yet

I can laugh about it now,
how foolish it is
to confuse

One passion
for another,
how easy,

To the extent of comprehension,
more or less, to confuse
the passion to love

With the passion to live.
She found me again,
years later,

She sought me out deliberately.
And I returned
with even more intention.

I left my husband.
I left our house.
I left the furniture,

The car,
the dog, the bird.
I took the child and ran

To her.
I ran to her.
How–

Foolish, I say again,
when we confuse
a passion to live

Means you must always
give up
something else.

It is not about women loving women
that is wrong, a mismatch,
against natural chemistries

Bodies that don't speak
each other's language.
Oh no.

But a story of a woman
who is her father's son,
the daughter

Who doesn't simply love her father,
makes him her hero,
but must be him

With other women.
She takes in
his finer qualities.

She protects like a perfect Amazon.
She knows
what a woman wants.

She adores her beloved, if not,
is adept at pretending.
The Daughter of the Father

Who is the son he never had,
a perfect clone of him,
except she knows how to love

Women,
unlike her father
who did not.

Sometimes, she imitates him too accurately.
Acting like a man is her own
aphrodisiac.

But thereby defeats the purpose
Of a woman being with a woman.
But *c'est la vie*, as Mamá Grande would have said.

It is the bargain we strike
with the goddesses above the Ninth Heaven,
what we give in exchange,

For veneration
of our flesh,
by a lover who lives solely

For our presence.
But I do not regret any of it,
and not the predictable.

Oh–
To find the same hand
played twice, this time on me,

Yes.
All I could do
was to love her more.

I found her
in our bed
with another woman,

A scene right out
of pulp fiction
when the hair pulling began.

The pungent odor
of cunt
and sweat,

Not in a *ménage à trois*,
not sexy at all,
not even remotely sensuous,

But beating each other
senseless.
I went for my child at the nursery,

With our suitcases
in the trunk,
his Ninja Turtles blanket and Power Rangers,

The box of Legos
to build a space station,
firehouse, a castle

In the air,
the little men,
the bitty children,

My alarm clock to get me up for work.
For a long time I adapted
to traveling light.

Just me
and him.
"Mama," he used to call me,

When he was a
bitty boy.
"Mama," he called me.

I learned to travel light
and like a good soldier,
under no conditions

When in the battlefront
must one
ever look back.

Or was that,
come to think of it, the litany
of Lot's Wife?

XIII. *El Hijo*

She was a self-created monument
to the Postmodern Woman as
Maternal Monster.

She frightened him.
She made him angry. No wonder
el hijo brooded all the time

She called him Byronic
tho' he wasn't quite sure
what that meant.

When she really lost it
she'd say he was a spoiled brat.
"You made me this way,"

Was his quick response, and
"I did not ask to be born,"
was another.

"How do you know?" she'd quip back
always faster than his draw,
no matter how the crew

He hung with admired his acumen.
They were not exactly *De Boyz from de Hood*,
but inner-city college men

Meaning they all had to work for their education,
restaurant bussers, twenty-four-hour
convenience store managers—like that.

Bound not by beliefs or convictions
but by an anti-politic,
born in the age of quantum physics,

That proclaimed nothing was what it was,
or where it was when you last saw it
and genetic engineering and technology

With the potential to end the class malaise
of Marx and Engels's age
but probably

Would not—
Capitalism,
like a stealthy rodent

Having the adaptability
to outwear
the Third World War—

The youth, therefore, did not see
any ground worth standing,
without first pointing out its contradictions.

And not even then.
Oh—
She was his mother.

She had done her job well enough.
She'd fed him.
Kept him clothed.

She saw to his schooling.
She had loved him,
too much perhaps.

As a child, he had been
the light of his mother's eyes,
she had spared him the paddle and scoldings,

Not so much as the wind—
the formidable *Ehecatl*—
was permitted to touch her boy.

And now, as a man on his own,
if something happened to him
who could prevent it, he thought.

Surely not *she* who was not
(he had discovered at around age five)
omnipotent.

And his father
(yes there was a father.
The boy wasn't the Immaculate Conception,

After all),
was even less so.
The father never came around anymore.

By adolescence,
raising another family somewhere,
he had made it clear

To the son
to make the effort
himself to be in touch.

But the mother,
Oh, the mother
never stopped.

Part Medusa,
part Mother Goose,
and part *Xochiquetzal*:

The Love Goddess
(tho', he as the son,
who had somehow managed

To slip right past the Oedipal stage,
preferred not to think of his mother's
dalliances and discreet liaisons).

Girls came easily.
At that age girls were always easy.
Until you let them know

You wanted them.
And when they wanted you,
you lost interest.

It seemed unnatural to be chased,
going against his predator's
instincts.

"Okay, *Bambi*,
so you've left the Enchanted Forest
and have gone to join the herd,"

The Gorgon Mother said,
who always had
something condescending

And obliquely terrifying
to say.
He used to be afraid of policemen

When he was a child.
They looked so tall and big.
But when he caught up in height

They were just men
doing a job
or not.

But this woman—
they had met head to head
when he was twelve.

Then he passed her right up
like a bamboo shoot
on a damp summer day.

She didn't care.
She stuck her finger high
in the air, right in his face,

The other hand at the waist.
They could be anywhere
and she'd give him

That stare,
that he read as a warning equivalent to the sign
in front of a nuclear power plant.

Only *she*
could do that to *him*.
Where was the umbilical cord buried

That once tied them,
before he was he
and she became *she,*

So that he could dig it up
and toss it into the sea.
Who had she scared before him?

Oh—
Intimidate
might be the better word

And not even that since
he'd left home,
he assured himself.

Now she would be just
a woman, like any other.
Women were intelligent.

He would never dispute it.
He preferred them assertive.
But something inside him

Somewhere rooted in the groin,
he suspected, and not in the neurons,
which is where he checked in

To verbally spar with friends,
professors,
his last boss at the computer store—

Of what else—
but the meaning of life.
When he talked to a woman

It was an internal and automatic
communication from brain
to pelvis.

Of course, he was all of
nineteen yet.
That was "normal,"

Or so everybody said.
Sometimes, although
without question not always,

His heart spoke right out
with its own language and instincts.
There were times now when

He did not know what to think.
He was all feeling
adrift

In a 3-D screen
of Plutonic glaciers
and Venusian heat.

El *cazador de corazones*
had outgrown Hesse and only paused
with *Crime and Punishment*.

He breezed through
Heidegger and Nietzche,
when he also drank up

Satie and Coltrane.
His mother had introduced him
to all of them

Not to mention Audre Lorde, Rich,
the usual suspects that showed up later
in his Woman's Studies Class,

And whose books
in original, tattered copies
he had found on the bookshelf

Next to his mother's bed,
along with vinyls and the shoeboxes
Of labeled cassette copies of classics.

By the time his crew
discovered Monk and Morrison,
Her son was bored with their brilliance

Spoon-fed on alternatives as he'd been
by a woman no bigger than his thumb
Who waved a magic wand

Between housework and a job,
where earning her modest pay
was not by anybody's measure

Minimally pleasant,
was not a vision of achievement.
Even to the lowly student that he was,

Who insisted on employment
which dignified his newly-honed mind
or else, he'd just not work.

Studying, after all,
was an acceptable vocation,
at least in the First World.

But he often wondered
how had the mother,
maid (at home and on the job),

Breadwinner
and "tolerator"
of the colorful parade

Of men and women
who passed through her life—
Found time to learn?

(They never talked
about her lovers,
not the men

Or the women,
but a child is the best observer
of a parent's private torments

And intuits with acute accuracy
the causes for misdirected impatience.)
But that was her business,

As he figured it,
having nothing to do
With the business of

Mothers and sons,
whose affinities
could not

Be denied,
like it or not.
Damn her, he said.

And damn her again.
(Since damnation meant nothing
To a godless man.)

Damn her agnosticism and her faith in him.
Other days when he was much less sullen,
it could be said, he marveled at the person

Who had set an example
of fortitude and tenacity,
if not to emulate than

At least to admire
(although it offered no advantage
to admit it).

Or the fact that he did enjoy her doting,
however it might embarrass him.
But especially he counted

As his good fate,
how the woman who bore him
had resolved to nurture something

That in and of itself
had done nothing to deserve it.
What more organic and without

Deliberate intention
(that he could fathom),
than to be brought forth

From her body
of blood and muscle,
contractions and expulsions?

Issued from between feces and urine,
according to Saint Augustine.
The Church of Peter and Paul

Had not seen woman's birthing
as extraordinary.
Nor had Jesus, apparently.

Why should they?
It was centuries
later

That the ovum was discovered.
Who knew Woman had made
any real contribution?

But not becoming a man
of religious leanings,
or in awe of any god,

El hijo de Ella
asked himself:
why should a Woman—

Who is neither
a vessel nor goddess—
not get up

And leave a newborn
to die in the bushes,
such a helpless

Creature
that had caused her
revolting pain

(As he had heard),
hardly human as it was
in those first moments?

What compelled her
to reach down
and embrace it—

Take it to her bosom
and let it thrive?
Unlike

The woman he heard about on the news,
who was seen bathing in the beach
after she had left her

Newborn
buried in the sand.
Inhuman

the authorities called her,
bitch,
not fit to be among the decent.

Lower
than a beast.
She should be outcast,

Stoned,
Imprisoned
for life.

But where
Oh—
Where was the male

Who had sired the infant?
Oh—
and where

Were those to prepare that woman
when she was pregnant,
to teach her

What society assumed,
demanded,
should not have to be taught?

Where—
the elder women
to fire up the *temazkal*

And cleanse the mother-to-be
with steam and herbs,
to recite the prayers that were to be said,

Sing the chants
that were good to be sung.
And where—the wise ones

For their age had brought experience
greater than all riches.
And the fathers, who were once

Brave and not as wise but still strong,
who brought gifts of rabbit and venison
to the post-partum woman?

Who were the leaders,
the priests and statesmen
that would guarantee the child's path?

Where were those who came to rejoice,
to bring offerings of fur and wool,
a cradle, a toy?

To the woman alone
there was nothing
but a haunting echo

Inside and all around, he was sure.
And he was glad
that he would never know it.

So there were days when he—
the son,
tho' aware, was often ridden

With black moods.
Was also relieved
that the woman

Who made him
had spared his life.
But now

It was up to him,
and no one else
to decide what to do with it.

XIV. Suicide

Once
her freshly-grown son,
her only own

Sprouting like the brightest of sunflowers,
spared of all grey and gloom,
or so she thought,

Although he was of this life
which was nothing, if not unforgiving
came to her and spoke of suicide.

They were an honest pair—
mother and son.
You had to give them that.

Well, she had too, often enough
thought of it.
A thought kept tucked

Under a pillow
and cast away in a dream.
It is the one freedom of all

Who have left childhood.
That's why it is so forbidden.
But because she loved him so

She selfishly talked him out of it.
Or maybe she didn't.
We still don't know.

In any case,
he didn't take his life then.
But some time after, she too,

Began to luxuriate in that
one freedom.
At first it came to her blithely,

The idea
of going back to paradise.
She had been there once

In a near-death experience
and knew that refuge
waited there.

With the son, freshly-grown
and therefore very much
without need of her

(As if he had ever been),
She had time, as they say,
for the devil's idle play.

Once, she had thought razors and tubs seemed such a mess.
And other ways when death came
were anything but a dignified exit.

Her own dead mother's lips bloated like a blowfish.
Her father's good looks, unrecognizable in a box.
And the voluptuous woman she once loved?

Her tongue—swollen like the obscene organ
that it was.
Oh—how unmerciful death was to the flesh.

Although, she had never loved the woman
with the swollen tongue.
But had only been seduced by her once—

Or almost.
(See how awful life is?
It does not grant

That love was ever true and real
even after death.
That is, if it were not.)

XV. *Mictlan*

"Someone is killing all the women,"
Elvira, who cleaned the high-rise
floors from one to thirteen,

Uttered between
bites of a bologna,
and processed cheese, diced jalapeños

Hold the mayo,
on *Pan Bimbo sanwiche*,
almost American

Her lunch was at eleven p.m.
Ella was on toilet duty
that week,

Like an unruly convict,
a bad Army recruit,
an unloved wife

Glutton for punishment,
or, as was the case: a worker
with a supervisor

Who made it clear one night:
union or not,
"If you don't put out,

"You can scrub the urinals
until your nails fall off and
your nose bleeds from the smell.

"Tell the management,
if you want to get fired.
I'll say

"I caught you smoking pot.
I'll call immigration
on your pals here.

"I don't care if you're
a citizen. I don't care
if you speak English.

"Get it straight.
To feed your kid,
you do what I say."

Twelve years of night cleaning.
Before that, while the boy
was small,

She stayed home with him and baby-sat
other people's children.
All day *huercos* screaming.

She went deaf
in one ear.
That's why a person reached middle age

Like a cat with nine lives,
that was patched and one-eyed.
It took that many to survive

The atrocities
of daily
banality.

Otherwise her health
was good.
"It has to be," she'd say,

Since there was no
insurance to speak of.
Just deductions

To pay
for bombs,
bursting prisons,

And other people's retirements.
It was how she saw it.
No apologies

To the politically correct.
The privileged
could worry about oil

Prices. She worried about
the gas bill.
Her son's college fees.

The fact that both
of her parents
died before age fifty

With bodies burned out
from lifetimes of produce picking.
And her youngest

Brother, stillborn,
without arms,
a result of her mother's

Exposure to pesticides sprayed
by crop dusters
as she labored below.

Hell was everywhere.
The Underworld was only
a matter of perspective.

"They are killing all the women
in Juárez," said Elvira again.
Now, she was smoking

A joint.
It was true
that they smoked pot.

But only on their breaks.
It helped dull the senses.
It kept

Her from the temptation
of doing something
unfortunate

And probably regrettable
to the supervisor,
but not from

Enjoying the fantasy
when she was
a little stoned.

What else she did
that she had not
done when she was young,

And strived to be the model
mother of the block,
which not just suburban housewives

Did, but underemployed single mothers
tried hard too,
was to fuck men half her age.

Well, back then, that would have made
them jailbait, anyway.
Not now.

Now they volunteered.
Happy recruits
who danced mambo

Like ballroom pros
out for the trophy.
They called her *Mamita*

And lied so sweetly
when she told them her true age,
not one for changing

What couldn't be changed.
They'd pucker their lips
and whistle low.

No way, they'd say.
If only their own mothers looked as fine.
If only the girl they got pregnant,

Or the virgin next door who
they wanted for a
wife.

Oh—
Oh—
Oh—

Teach me tonight,
Like Etta James would sing.
Another thing

Ella did to keep from going
insane
from such an overflow of sudden sadness

Was to pretend she was white.
No.
She did not tell people that.

She did not talk *Fun with Phonics.*
She'd sit in a corporate café,
and act like she

Had nothing else to do
but to annoy people, sipping
a five dollar cup of coffee

While chatting loudly on a cell phone.
The mobile wasn't hers.
She had found it

On the sidewalk.
It wasn't even connected.
She just made things up.

She laughed,
pretending to choke on something funny
when she reached the bottom of the recyclable cup.

She bought the *New York Times*,
and always disgusted
with the headlines,

She'd leave it behind,
like she couldn't have used it
to wipe the mirrors and windows at home.

Oh, something else.
It was Matías,
the *indio* from Iztapalapa,

With features like a pre-classic *Tlatilco* figurine.
He was not like the other young men.
Él la adoraba de veras.

Years came and went,
and there was nothing
he wouldn't do to please

Within his means,
which were, it should be stressed,
limited.

He ran her bath,
polished her toenails and detailed her car.
Things like that.

Or for instance, she'd ask,
"Am I fat?"
A woman's ultimate test

Of loyalty.
"No," he'd say, "You're perfect."
And she would spare him another day.

With all the tips from moving furniture
he took her out on the town.
Once a tart waitress

Tried to be smart.
"And what can I get your son?"
she asked,

Referring to Matías.
And *Ella*, without blinking
said, "Don't be foolish.

My son
is so much better-looking.
And if *you* were,

I'd introduce you to him."
Matías was a tourniquet
and kept her from bleeding to death.

XVI. *Tonalli*

To the ancient ones
Tonalli
meant a child came into this world

With his own destiny.
But even so, a man could will it away,
rise above or fall below.

The problem was
that destiny was all around
and suffocating.

So the child once grown,
might never have a chance,
or even see it coming.

I was named after my *tío* Matías.
Escorpión—
is what they called my brother on the street

Because his bite was deft and mean.
He was killed in a knife fight
when he was barely twenty-one.

Mamá, who was the oldest,
had already had us,
my two siblings and me.

Our father was in *el Norte*.
After the murder and no justice,
she said, "That's it."

The next time my father phoned
from the place called Chicago,
Mamá told him, "Get ready for us."

And we were on our way.
The way of thousands.
Some make it, some don't.

You've read the news.
Surely, you've seen it on *Telemundo*.
How the *coyotes* pack us like sardines

In death traps on wheels.
How they leave us wandering in the desert
like deranged Jews

Searching for the Promised Land.
No, that's us.
The one-celled organisms

At the bottom of the food chain
that nevertheless—
Oh,

Not for a minute,
should anyone be mistaken,
that it is not us—

Who have made this country
what it is.
My great-grandfather worked

The railroads during the days of
Porfirio Díaz or should I say decades?
My grandfather was a *bracero*.

He traveled all the way to
Toledo, Ohio.
That's where he met *Abuela*

Antonia Cruz. She was Indian,
too. In my *familia* we don't
pretend. We're not

Mixed blood. There are no buried
Spanish titles beneath
anyone's tombstone.

Our ancestors are not signed
in the Church's registry.
They all got baptized at once;

Worse, were sent for life to mine or plow
and plant and hoe.
Our gods and temples destroyed.

Then they took memory,
a mass lobotomy,
mental genocide.

Their grit, sweat,
brawn and backs
made into preindustrial cyborgs.

Don't talk to us
of mysticism
in Teotihuacan—

An archaeological zone
turned into a New Age park.
Don't talk to the people of Iztapalapa,

Of New Fire ceremonies
and rescuing Aztec rites to the Sun
from the past

For the sake of the polluted present,
where their boom box
and graffiti descendants

Make up their own customs
recited in hip-hop verses
to heavy metal rock.

And all they want is out.
Those of polite society
like their Indians in feathers,

They like us with rattles made of
gourds.
They like us noble.

Most of all, they want us peaceful.
But where I come from,
an armpit of *La Capital,*

Even the air is violent
and the sky wretched.
The earth, once fertile,

"Not even to mention,"
fallow where there
isn't asphalt.

Centuries of poverty in Iztapalapa
have done away with nearly
all courtesies and pretensions.

Doña Antonia was the only
one who didn't come
from the village of my *gente,*

Swallowed up as it was by the
biggest metropolis outside
of Hong Kong. We are probably

More in numbers than the Chinese.
That's a lot
of cheap labor.

My mamá
worked in a *maquiladora*
along the Tijuana border

Until my father and grandfather
sent us enough to cross over.
It cost a thousand

A head. Me, I was ten,
my two sibs and of course,
Mamá. The *coyote*

And his cronies took us
through a huge sewage pipe.
It was huge to me then.

It stunk like all get-out.
By the time we got to the Other Side,
we were in *los Estados.*

A truck was waiting for us.
There were about eleven *pollos* in total.
"Keep the kid in front,"

Someone said. The kid was me.
I could see. I could breathe.
The rest rode in the bed.

They were stretched out
one lying on top of the other.
"I thought I was going to die

Then and there," my mother said
after. "But later," she said,
"I really wanted to die."

She doesn't talk about the rape.
My sister told me about it.
My sister was fourteen

And on her period the whole
time. She bled right through
her jeans. My brother,

The eldest, says he doesn't remember
any of it. He's blocked it out.
Post-traumatic stress

They call it. His whole life
with a psychologist
and taking medication.

He hates my father. There
was a woman living with our dad
when we got here,

Whom he moved out but kept
in another place.
Oh, yes. I left out some details

About the trip. Just a few.
We were caught and sent back twice
before we finally made it to L.A.

I remember running like a pack
of stray dogs along the freeway.
Can you imagine that sight

To anyone driving past? Like—
What was that?
Us.

Among the millions
who come to keep things going.
Put the strawberries on dinner tables

In midwinter.
Landscape front yards and gardens
without much haggling in case

You get mad and call immigration.
In restaurants, we don't offend customers
by taking their orders

But are hired only
to keep the water glasses filled.
We wash the dishes of America.

We wash hotel linen, cars, people's babies.
We'll clean anything.
Whatever dirty job, in other words,

That has to be done is ours for the asking.
How else to explain why we find
work when the economy is down

And unemployment lines keep growing?
Must have something to do with the lack
of benefits a godforsaken *cabrón* must live with.

Arabs and South Africans drive taxis.
Asian Indians run motels.
The East and Middle East

Have major stick-togetherness—
legacies of tribal clans and family dynasties,
a birthright to their ancestors,

Traced to the land of their kin,
that helps each one get ahead.
Our support system is just that:

"Help me get to the Other Side
to work
myself to death."

Just because I know
how the system runs, doesn't mean
I can do anything about it.

My father had some ingenuity.
He bought a truck
and started a moving business.

That's who I work with—
my father.
My mother ended up leaving him.

The drinking
would have been enough reason
But then she found out about the gringa.

Here's how it goes for me then:
You won't catch me with a white woman.
And I don't have much use for alcohol.

I don't even smoke. One girlfriend
called me a mama's boy.
I design clothes.

The men in my family say I must be gay.
I took my mother's sewing machine and taught myself.
It's not all about moving furniture

And watching soccer games on cable.
It's not all about what women to score
on payday. "Life is not a pissing contest,"

I tell my brother-in-law.
"Why not?" He laughs.
My sister deserves better.

At least I thought until she made a comment
about the woman I'm with.
I met her

At the boutique where they take
my designs on consignment.
She compared me to Saint Laurent.

"No, I'm San Juan," I said.
San Juan is my patron saint—
Saint John the Baptist.

I also pray to San Juan de Letrán
and Saint John the Apostle.
I pray to all the *Juanes*.

You have to believe something
believes in you.
She asked me to make a dress

Just for her.
Size eight petite.
She didn't even ask how much.

A lot of class, I thought. My
first true fan. Then I watched
her walk away.

Any questions anybody ever had
about my manhood ended
that day.

Allow me to correct myself.
Let me escort out the not-so-enlightened
aspects of my culture

That I love—
that I'm proud of—
that I'll carry to my grave—

No matter where I end up living—
no matter how rich or famous—
I may or may not ever get—

And say that you don't have to be straight
to be a man.
I'm not a Neanderthal

Like my *cuñado* who thinks if you are not
chasing a new conquest
you must be dead.

But I don't talk about *her* much at all,
whom I keep like a spinning doll
in an organza gown

Inside a music box.
I let her out for my eyes only,
waltzing to *Für Elise*.

Ella
who made the dress look like a million
that I put together

Like a frantic genie
under duress.
And then I made another

And the third one became a gift
for Christmas. She invited me
over. We had a glass of wine

And slow danced to the quiet
snow falling outside.
Es la historia de un amor.

Ours.
"We," I say,
 only when she's not around.

"She's older than Mamá,"
clucked my sister,
pointing out the obvious,

Who has been cuckolded more
times than she can count
and does not understand that faithfulness

Doesn't depend on social requisites
of appropriateness, like age or status,
but on knowing what you want

And recognizing it,
if you are lucky enough
to have found it.

But in this case,
however true it was about her age,
she did not look like my mother.

She did not look
like anyone's mother.
She had fast and hard rules.

She turned you into a gentleman
and a feminist in a few tough lessons.
Soccer has nothing over her.

The Sport of Keeping
a Woman Like Her Content
would be a real macho's challenge.

Sometimes
I want to give it all up.
Even her.

I'm not a slacker.
Don't get me wrong.
What would I do in New York

Or L.A.
much less in Paris or Rome?
A penniless Chocolate Man

Without contacts.
What runway show would have me?
Who—besides a few acquaintances with storefronts—

Would ever give me a break?
Then I go see to see *her*
to whine

Like a drama queen,
like someone picked
for Reality TV,

With porcelain-capped teeth,
who looks good in cut-offs
and whose biggest problem

Is eliminating all the rest
of the contestants who look just like me
and who act like me, and

Who look and act just like all
of America wished they could
look and act like

So that if I win
I can make it
as a no-talent celebrity

For five minutes,
Warhol genius.
I forget

The night she has just had
scrubbing office toilets
until I feel a good swift kick

In the ass
that sets me back
on track again.

That's about
as romantic
as she gets.

XVII.   In the Jaws of *Xolotl*

At work, Elvira always made sandwiches.
She'd bring chocolates
and crème-filled cupcakes

In cellophane wrapped packages
that neither of them
could open once

They were high.
"How do you know
they are killing the women

In Juárez?"
She asked.
"Going on four hundred,"

Elvira replied instead,
"For ten years and still the
numbers go up.

"There are all kinds of theories
But bottom line—
No one cares.

"They said it was a rich Egyptian.
Bus drivers have been blamed, too,
and satanic cult members

Who stalk
thin-boned young women
on their way to work or school,

"Mexican, each one.
Ay–comadre, I don't mean
just by culture or language

"But by blood.
They work in *maquiladoras*
like slaves

"For a few bucks a day.
Or they are schoolgirls
or children.

"The youngest was five.
But they were all brown.
They were poor.

"And to me, that's the core
of why no one cares.
You know it.

"And I know it."
Elvira, whose back ached,
and shoulders

And arms,
and feet,
slumped down in a chair

That by morning
belonged to an executive,
who pissed cocaine

Or Prozac. Elvira went on,
"My cousin worked in a
maquiladora.

"She made shoelaces
for the Nikes
brought from Indonesia,

"Or put the buttonholes on Gap clothes.
Don't sue me, I only
suppose.

"It could be anything
anyone wears anywhere
in the world today.

"That's how I know
about the unsolved murders.
Two of her companions

"Were found in a garbage dump.
They were stripped.
They were tortured.

"I am telling you
someone is killing the women.
They are found mutilated.

"They die in the most horrible way.
It's a Jack the Ripper case,
only worse.

Can someone tell the presidents—
both this one
and that one—

"That they are not surplus or waste?
Brown girls
with no way to defend themselves

"And no one to
write so much as a letter
on their behalf.

"Or maybe it is drug cartels
with money to burn
and sadistic tastes.

"Or organ dealers like scavengers
on the prowl
that include the *coyotes*

"Who are paid
to smuggle the victims over.
Who knows?"

Elvira was right to say it again.
Who really cared about poor brown women
who died

Like the daughters of Demeter
to bring winter
to a place hotter than hell.

Xolotl was elected of all the
sixteen hundred gods of the Aztecs
to bring back the souls from *Mictlan*.

But it was *Xolotl*,
grotesque underworld god
who stole *Xochiquetzal*,

Queen of Spring and Beauty,
Goddess of love
and carried her down.

He ravished her there.
He licked her bones clean.
A psychopath of a deity.

Who came up with these things?
Priests who pricked their genitals
with thorns,

Who hallucinated
with peyote or *hongos* or
fresh blood they drank from

The "Christs" that they
sacrificed.
After winter, *Xochiquetzal* returned

To Paradise,
and like Eve, she tasted
the fruit of its tree

And was expelled.
So began autumn.
Such simpler a tale of seasons

Than a doctrine of religion
that condemned
everyone earnest enough

To have faith
or was born
into a religion, if it wasn't a race.

Oh, they were killing
the women,
and I had three and a half hours left to go—

She and I and Elvira
with her false Social Security card.
Elvira from Chihuahua,

Another no man's land,
where now
the serial murders had spread.

But no one mourned
the dead
who died again in hell,

And no one heard
my gleeful laugh
minute as Tinkerbell's,

To know that I was just two paychecks away
from ascending
via a single spider's thread

Climbing
on Lucifer's shoulders
back to heaven.

Or, if you preferred,
the New World version instead:
clasped in *Xolotl*'s jaws.

Or for the social realist:
in a soap opera
for the disenfranchised,

It would have been
Matías's dark, skinny arms,
Tezcatlipoca strong,

God of Black Night,
Double Meanings
and Good Fortune.

But like Elvira said:
who cared who or what
inadvertently helped me to escape?

He would never get to see the moon.
Cipactli—
oceanic dragon,

Would banish each and every one.
I was there before the beginning.
And I would be there after the end.

XVIII. Righteous White Boyz

Maybe the last generation of their kind:
Red diaper babies spoon-fed liberal politics
and the rebellious offspring of bigoted parents.

The Nineties ushered in retro-fifties politics
disguised as economic prosperity for all.
And Righteous White Boyz were looking for their place.

They penned provocative articles on human rights
in college bulletins to inflame the dean, joined
Habitat for Humanity or spent a year in the Peace Corps.

In Honduras they sent out electronic missives
about twenty-three hours around the clock in sweatshops,
disseminated information with the fervor

Of the last Western reporter behind the Iron Curtain
when there was an Iron Curtain,
and when there were communists to join or fight,

When Russia was still united
and China was mean and closed tight.
For Righteous White Boyz who knew no boundaries

No borders were prohibited.
They ate grubs traveling through South Africa,
kept the steady diet of the locals in Indonesia,

Survived fevers from the water or pork tacos in Reynosa.
To clinch their third world qualifications
the Righteous White Boyz fell in love

With mulattas during Mardi Gras
and stayed with them a season in favelas,
wondering but not wondering where

Destitute black girls went at night.
Or they crossed downtrodden Vietnam villages
with back pack and a *Lonely Planet* guide.

Feeling like the Last White Guy on the planet.
They stayed with families of the disappeared
in Chile, Argentina or El Salvador

Who were still disappeared after they left.
Back home no matter for whom they voted
or for whom they did not,

No matter how loud the rallies they joined
and how many times they were dragged off
or pepper sprayed by the enemy cop.

No matter how black and po' they talked when
poor and black folk were around,
no matter what they said or did,

It was her opinion and would remain so
all her life that a Righteous White Boy
could never know what it was,

What it had been and would be for a long time ahead,
to be in the brown woman's skin.
No matter the country or citizenship

She knew what they otherwise never would—
that brown, poor and female
was what it was.

They did not, for example, get letters from a cousin
in a Texas prison who had been gang recruited
and ended up in jail for life before

He was old enough to drive.
They were not brown mothers of brown boys
that only with luck and determination

Would reach adulthood alive,
when they'd then have to deal with being brown men—
something else that White Boyz could not know firsthand.

She could have been the Poster Girl
for all that was wrong with the nation just before
the turn of the century

When a solid (tho' questionable in size) chunk
of the population felt it was doing fine.
But *Ella* was from another time

And very much done with it.
She was past the days of union meetings
and CP members passing out pamphlets outside factories.

She was past being intimidated by both foremen
and union stewards. Unions as a concept
were in and of themselves of the past.

Yet how those 'funky white boys' loved
to come around and proselytize.
And after a night or two, they loved even more

To call themselves her boyfriend, lover,
or if they were really not shy about it—
Compañero, bien Pos-Sandinista,

Loaded with *conscientización* and
practicing their Spanish on her.
Unlike snotty White chicks who were concerned

About diamond rings and nannies
White Boyz could exhaust their charm
On the Third World going Dutch on dates

And at home washing dishes
after the meals they prepared together,
thereby proving they were more feminist

Than the Seventies radical feminists, *oye.*
Overcompensating, just maybe,
for the privileged education

From the CEO father who still paid their rent,
or the divorced mother who had raised them
on a teacher's salary.

These self-righteous lover boys just could not know
no matter how far or how close they got
what it was to dream and know you were only dreaming.

They loved her, they said, especially at night
and in the dark with a rapture
that scared them both—

Even if only for the moment
it seemed so real—
the idea of it.

They didn't mind Mexican chicks,
tho' they tended to be quiet
And not as culturally hip as the Asian Indian,

Without the cache of being Native American
or to cause the eyeball dilating effect of the sight
of a Moroccan, hands painted with cinnabar.

Righteous White Boyz loved to fuck
Brown, Yellow, Red,
former Soviet Union White

But especially Black girls.
The blacker the better (even a little nappy-haired,
And don't think that a Righteous White Boy

Would not call a woman on a weave.)
They were downright capable of simulating worship
only if she remained authentically oppressed.

It did not cross their thick cabezaheads
that such a woman just might not like
to see herself or be thought of as a victim.

As much as they loved the idea of *la Otra*–
dark woman as primal symbol of true courage
and indomitable strength.

To be able to lift her up
like a mudbug from a griddle,
was the only kind of female worthy of his conviction.

XIX. The Archivist

His life was books, Miller's was.
No one called him by his Christian name.
No one knew it.

He preferred it that way,
protocol and etiquette having gotten
lost among the commoners.

He wasn't royalty.
He just thought of himself
as if he were.

He imagined
as a child
that he had been kidnapped

By gypsies
in Minneapolis
while his father

The king
of a very far off land
on the "Continent"

Traveled on business.
His life was spent
researching

People's histories,
Any, but his own.
He would have wanted to be

An explorer,
a marine biologist,
a lion trainer,

But his father
(Not the king of his
boyhood fantasies

But the ex-Marine
who had raised him)
harsher than any lion trainer

Had raised his boys with an iron fist.
He broke their spirits
with his Marine lifer's

Sense of discipline,
his medals,
which he had them

Polish to a sheen
and his own youth
in the orphanage

That plagued him,
and running away to the war
against the "Japs and Kikes."

As for the mother
of the Archivist,
she hung herself

Before he knew her.
Ultimately,
with more degrees than he

Knew what to do with
all Miller could manage
was to organize,

To make sure
things were
in their place.

At home it was the kitchen cabinets,
his library,
the shoes and coats in closets,

Ties arranged by color,
folded socks in perfect order
in the drawer.

At work it was papers
filled with such glorious stories
that took up the hours

But never made a sound,
not the tiniest disruption
to blaspheme the peace

And an individual's right
to hear himself
think.

But when someone did come along
abrasive or loud, an unruly child
or a cantankerous old person with his

Arthritic dog,
surely both ridden with disease
Oh—

The irony.
How the Archivist forgot
the disdain he grew up with,

And he'd send them quickly away.
The world was filled with nasty
humanity from which all he wished

Was to disassociate.
One day
she wandered in

Smelling of what he thought
was an essence that came close
to nostalgia.

But on second consideration,
perhaps were pheromones—
Invisible, odorless design of Mother Nature,

Female inbred ensnarement
of the opposite sex
for the sake of reproducing the race.

And he would have no part of it.
Oh—
But still the scent

Of her lingered
with him for days.
It stayed in his herringbone jacket.

He smelled it on his cuffs,
Although she'd never gotten
close enough to touch.

The third time she came by
he said he loved her.
It came out just like that,

And unleashed a rush
of such inane chatter on his part
such that it startled him

As much as it did her.
He went on all night long.
He had never talked so much to anyone.

Not even to his therapist
of the last nine years.
If only she would marry him.

If only she would agree
to live together.
But she had a son, she said.

And remembering how he hated
his father who had hated his sons
and not just did not know

How to love them,
as would have been understandable
given his own unfortunate

Early abandonment,
the Archivist immediately
hated the boy

Whose mother
would choose him
over the love of a good man.

For surely he was good.
At least he had no bad intentions
that he was aware of,

That might surface,
such as a degrading reversion
to a childhood trauma.

He might, for instance, wake up,
huddled in a corner,
or having wet the bed.

But this woman
was saving her compassion
for her child,

Who being a child—
he was convinced—
was selfish as all children were,

And could not ever deserve it
as he, Miller, would have.
If only she had thought

To give herself to him.
He (unlike children,
who had nothing to give in return)

Could have made it worth her while.
He had insurance benefits,
a pension plan. He had a little house

With a walnut tree.
He would have given up his den
to make room for the kid.

But no, she said.
No, the second time he asked, too.
And then, she stopped coming in.

XX. The Seminarian

"Divine Vengeance"
he called the consequence
of his mother's broken promise,

A spiritual crisis that he carried
since birth,
earliest memory, at least,

And which kept him from
marrying until
he was forty.

She had pledged
to dress the scrawny
runt—last of her dozen children,

As the Holy Infant
if the child survived his first year.
Miraculously,

The baby grew healthy,
even fat.
The mother

Forgot her pledge.
Or more than likely
had no money to sew fine fabrics

Like the ones on the saints in Church
with German lace trimming and crimped,
such as the work of spinsters

Who had no children
to feed,
to dress,

No men of their own
who would command
their time,

Wear out their bodies,
and fade their beauty and youth.
The mother

With so much
on her hands figured
God would understand.

The Seminarian spent his adult life
questioning.
Doubts simply plagued him.

They followed him
like personal mascots,
like the sparrows

Painted
on the shoulders of
Saint Francis.

A spiritual angst
that made him writhe,
drenched in a sweat of prayers

For deliverance,
the unending quest of man's
search for reunion

With God—ever his passion,
pure source
worthy of his love

And wish for wholeness.
Having no recollection
of his beginnings

Or a desire to return to the earth.
Oh—
But how men had yearned

For enclosed
places—
such as from whence they came:

Cathedrals with high domed ceilings,
temples with embracing arches,
the *indio's* teepee,

The sweat lodge
of dried deerskins
and volcanic rocks,

Where you entered
on all fours in the dark
and folded into a fetus,

Spoke
directly to God,
Who spoke back

In the sound of a drum.
A God ever present in the form
of Father and Mother

That cared for
His and Her children,
a God that brought on the rain

And relieved man's anguish,
the pain that flowed
through the uteruses of all women.

The Seminarian
fell in love when it came to him
that he would one day die

And die alone.
But the woman he chose,
a radiant near-virgin

Who sang in the choir,
left him
not long after the wedding.

The loneliness she bore
in their marriage, the constant silence
that passed for sacred contemplation,

And fervent solicitations
for confirmation
of God's approval

Of their love
was more
than any blonde from Maryland

With a promising career
could take,
one year into the third millennium.

The Seminarian,
who of course,
had long since left the seminary

(Yet saw himself perpetually
as a candidate
on the Church's doorstep),

Was left to doubt all the more.
Oh—but how marvelous
the fruit of that doubt—

To taste its bitterness again,
to bathe in its salty waters,
to drink its brine of vinegar and peppers.

The doubt of the lonely man,
draped like a vest of horse hair,
that chafed and bled the flesh,

A penitent's flagellating crawl
up to Golgotha:
Place of a Skull.

Was most certainly
the Almighty's
mercy.

Then, one day
when the divorce began
to feel real

He became
aware
of *her*—

A wash
of dusk rose and aquamarine
on coarse *amate* paper—

Casually at first, he noticed
her, a stone
along his labyrinthine walk—

Through what most
see as life
and he,

As a passing through,
a test,
something to be endured—

A stone,
that nevertheless grew
into a boulder

The more he tried
to avert his attention
in the office,

Just as she started
her shift,
and he worked late.

What temptations
woman
brought with or without her knowing,

At least that one,
with her crow's feet laughter
and naïve disposition.

Naïve as any person
ignorant
of her own mortality,

Especially one
of such humble
background.

Naïve,
as any woman
he didn't know.

He only knew
that which he imagined
beneath her dress

When she bent
to empty the wastebasket,
the curve of her fine arms

As she pushed the vacuum cleaner
back and forth
rhythmically down the hall,

Until she became a shadow
and divided in two.
She, with the noisy apparatus

And the silhouette
she cast on the wall.
While he perceived himself

As nothing,
not so much as vapor,
since no one

Perceived him at all.
Then came the night
he stayed

With every intent
to wait and watch for that one
whose slender neck had a tiny black mole

Just to the left peeking
through her hair,
which she refused to wear up

Under a cap, as did the others,
or wrapped inside a net,
so vain was she, no doubt.

And yet, that made her
all the more
appealing.

The evening he took her,
(he thought later,
she may have taken him,

So quick did she respond),
without a word between them.
Not then,

Not during
and not after.
He grew tense

As time passed,
ridden with repentance.
On Sunday,

He did not attend Mass.
At night he stopped reading scriptures
before bed.

The unavoidable occasion came
when they met up again,
He, working late,

She, starting her shift,
and seeing the light on
she peered in.

She did not greet him,
as once she had,
with what he then thought

Was respect and deference,
But what may have been
disdain instead.

But how could she have hated him?
What had he done to deserve it?
Was it that he took

What was freely given,
and she had wanted more
from him?

Why did women
always
want more?

She stared
and he met her gaze
expectant of the recrimination

That she would surely hurl.
And he would take it.
What other recourse did he have?

It was a cavalier's duty.
And he would tell her
of his remorse,

Offer
something
in compensation.

Friendship, perhaps.
Then, without flinching,
the lips—

He once searched for
in the darkness,
with such ardor

Oh— and
kissed
to a feverish pitch —

Parted coolly,
and she asked,
"Señor,

would you like
for me
to empty your trash?"

XXI. Baggage

They couldn't live in more different worlds,
coinhabiting the same city tho' not—
the same street.

In 2003,
neighborhoods still counted for something.
Bill lived Downtown.

In Chicago—which it went without saying,
was not New York, and while we are at it,
not L.A., Houston or Santa Fe,

But an old American city with exceptionally
tall buildings. American, meaning,
in this case, full of everything that

Came this way from everywhere else in the world.
The price for the view from very tall buildings
cost a good American buck.
She had met Bill that night,
lived on the thirty-eighth floor right
next to the Tribune Building.

He needed a maid.
Not a clean glass in sight.
His condo was mostly a large living area with

A spectacular sight of the Lake.
He had very few possessions.
That made sense, no room.

Where would I keep my shoes, to start with?
—she asked herself, when he invited her up
for a drink.

Not that she was moving in.
And no, she was not there
by mistake, or

As a call girl or
to clean up,
but actually, for once, as a guest, in such a place.

They met at a wedding reception.
Safe enough for chance meetings, those days,
when everyone was getting married.

Old, young, second time around posting
announcements in the paper like blushing virgins,
everyone—

A Brave New World frenetic coupling
to secure a reservation before the Ark sailed off.
Everyone, that was, but her.

She would rather be shot,
in the head,
three times—

She said to her friends.
"If I even mention it,
and then, am too chicken to pull the trigger,

Which would be a very good possibility,
do me the favor, please.
Don't worry. I'll sign a euthanasia waiver."

Her friends consented,
without any questions.
They were very loyal.

"Or,"
rethinking the scene for the homicide squad,
her son,

Who would be called in to identify her bloody remains,
Or,
if he could not be found,

Like most times when she needed him lately,
some long lost good for nothing
relative or, even the ex-husband,

People who just might,
in a morbid way, find pleasure in her demise,
she thought, poison might work best,

Administered organically by way
of a tiny serpent,
like Cleopatra had her maidservants deliver,

Yes.
She often spent time reading up on such events
just in case.

Meanwhile, people were
getting married everywhere,
it seemed, as of late,

Or maybe, it had been happening for
a very long time, but now, the tricky part was that
there was an unprecedented and serious

Disproportionate ratio
of women to men—of all ages—
worldwide.

Now,
a few gay men were helping to even out
the gender disparity by coming out of the closet

Instead of taking up a woman's reproductive years
to produce their heirs,
keeping up appearances at work

And family gatherings,
trying their best to look good for the world,
for the last few millennium,

And, meanwhile, sneaking around,
there were just not enough lesbians to pick up
the plethora.

Then,
there were women
like her—

Oh—
too many for some,
too few to go around for others.

An aberration for most.
And when she surfaced,
like a rumored Siren,

Mothers and fathers,
hide your children!
Kin of every background,

Preferred not to think,
of such a woman's other life.
Instead, they called her

A spinster, or she did the family a favor
and went into the convent early on,
or signed up for ministry work in Somalia,

Or, became "a career girl"
who couldn't be bothered with
a husband and children.

Yes,
That was it.
Such women couldn't be bothered.

Or,
she was an artist.
Everyone had heard of the bohemians of Paris,

The debauchery of the decadent.
Yes,
that was what artists did.

"Do you want water with your scotch?" Bill asked.
(He'd rinsed out two cups he took out
of the loaded dishwasher.)

She didn't know.
She never drank scotch.
She hadn't smoked cigarettes for a long time, either,

But there she was doing it,
smoking Bill's Marlboros.
What a disgusting habit, she thought,

Lighting up another, she was celebrating
the view that she had never enjoyed before.
She'd seen it for years when she worked cleaning offices.

But not like this.
(Don't let anyone tell you, at least
she would not after that night,

That the city you got from high up
was the same city
you got on the ground.)

Bill's golf clubs were by the door.
He also played tennis and racketball.
He belonged to the Downtown Athletic Club.

What a jock.
So fit and so tanned.
Impressive.

She bet he even got his back
waxed.
Plus,

He was well-
traveled.
Things were looking up for Bill.

He talked about his business trips
and vacations
(on which, for a fleeting moment, she thought

He might one day invite her along).
And the boat.
There was the summerhouse in Michigan

That his wife got in the divorce.
The fishing trips to Belize had to stop
when the son got accepted at Princeton.

Their youngest daughter
was getting married
next spring.

And with each revelation
of Bill's recent past seeping into his present
Ella—

Imagined clearly,
not just the man's baggage—so to speak—
piling up before them,

But a whole set of matching luggage,
monogrammed *y* special ordered,
ready to go—

Whenever they'd meet (if they ever would)
Or talk (if he ever called)
Again.

Yes.
Bill's dark-eyed Latin fantasy,
began to feel the view from the thirty-eighth floor

Somewhat nauseating by the time
she finished the drink and he sat
next to her with the bottle.

She found her shoes
(that while they were not designer
or expensive,

Or even the latest fashion),
still showed off
nice feet,

Which was first and foremost
the important thing.
Or at least, that was what a woman told herself,

A mantra to get by in America,
América,
I wanna be in América,

When she couldn't afford what she'd rather wear.
Shoes aside and no
closet space to put them in anyway,

She found her acrylic *rebozo,*
and made for the door.
"Don't go, hon'…!

All I wanna do
is talk,"
Bill-with-the-Baggage called out,

As if that were something
that she—
who did not stop,

or so much
as wave good-bye—
did not know.

XXII. Dangerously Happy

"Then I found out
that these were my assets,"
Lisbeth said,

Cupping each of her breasts
and lifting them,
as if she were weighing melons.

Lisbeth came from
Lebanon
by way of *la Capital*—

El D.F.
Mexico City,
twenty-one-million strong

And still growing.
Chilangos they call themselves.
Lisbeth was one hundred percent Chilanga,

One hundred percent believer in
Our Lady of Guadalupe.
One hundred percent Lebanese.

One hundred percent Muslim.
One hundred percent still in an arranged marriage.
And one hundred percent *loca*.

Oh – what I could not tell you about her
that wouldn't tingle your toes.
Lisbeth

With hair that fell in undulations
like a glazed Niagara Falls.
Her gold bangles from wrist to elbow

And rhinestone belt jangling
when she belly-danced
at the restaurant

Where I washed dishes
and threw out the trash,
and swept and mopped the kitchen floor,

And sprayed for roaches,
and set the rat traps,
and made sure there was always

Soap in the dispenser
and toilet paper
in the bathrooms,

And once was almost electrocuted
when the *deficiente* manager
told me to get the blender going or else,

In the midst of some big quiche order
or who knows what,
everyone running around

Like we were Maxim's,
and I tried to fix the cord by biting
down on the exposed wires

With my teeth
just as one of the bussers was plugging it in
trying to be helpful

And the manager told me I was lucky
he didn't fire me for that.
I eventually quit.

So did Lisbeth.
To keep up our new friendship
we'd sometimes meet for a drink.

Once, after our third vodka tonic
she told me that
if I really painted,

If I were really serious about it,
she would bring her lover over
to see my "work."

"It's not work,"
I said.
God.

How could the only thing I did
that brought me
pleasure,

That let me relax,
that sent me
far

Oh—I do mean,
far away
from everything else I did,

Be work?
Work
was scrubbing pots the size

Of small metal bathtubs.
Work was trying to figure out
algebra equations

To help my son with his homework.
Work was the hideous curtains I made
that ended up too short for the windows

But that at least kept out some of the winter's draft.
But work
was most definitely not

Painting
on paper of fine grain
when and if I allowed myself

To splurge on it.
Sometimes,
for Christmas

I'd go downtown
and spend the whole afternoon
selecting art supplies at the store,

Only that which fell within the budget, of course.
So, I had to select carefully and well,
like a housewife on market day,

Squeezing every avocado, lime and pepper,
until she got just the right one.
I'd come home and wrap each brush,

Resplendent oils, a new palette—
Once I bought an easel.
I put a big bow on it and left it by the tree

Until the twenty-fifth.
"What're you waiting for," *Mi'jo*
asked, knowing himself

What his presents were, too,
since I couldn't afford to go wrong,
he'd also pick out his own.

Lisbeth took off her glasses
and held them up against the light.
She was blind as a bat.

She wiped them with the edge
of her leopard-print see-through blouse,
with ruffle sleeves.

"This guy has a gallery or something.
No,
I think he's on a board of some sort

With the Contemporary Art Museum.
I don't really know him.
But I got his attention,

"If you know what I mean.
He's the one that got me out of
stripping."

(This was when
strip bars
were dark, seedy places,

Where doing a lap dance
broke a woman's spirit so bad,
she'd have to be on heroin first.)

Don't kid yourself,
sticking her pussy
in a stinking stranger's face

Can hardly be any woman's
idea
of fun.

Lisbeth said she once threw up
on the bar-top just from the smell
of one john's breath.

Oh yeah,
that was another thing.
Stripping

Was a synonym
for cheap prostitution.
The owner and bouncers

Got their cuts.
Lisbeth
wrote novels on the side.

They all took place
in Mexico City,
in the fancy District of Polanco.

The protagonist was a platinum
blonde
like Lisbeth.

Yeah.
Blonder than Shakira–
before Shakira,

Long before.
Why not?
Who can invent anything new

In the Third Millennium?
Lisbeth and I would meet
at the Redhead Piano Bar.

Ella–
la morena
Lisbeth, *la güera libanesa*

Never accepted any drinks
that were sent over.
They/we just went to talk

With each other.
You know,
like friends.

It's what friends
do,
even women like us.

Like us, alone.
Lisbeth's story was unfettered
by family,

Like mine was.
She had left everyone behind,
although she was married to an engineer

Who had taken a job with a company
outside Chicago.
He'd kept her locked in the house.

It had all the amenities,
including a maid
from Poland,

Who came to clean every day.
One day Lisbeth asked permission
to go shopping for a new dress,

Maybe shoes to match,
a purse,
"Yes," he said,

"Get whatever you want.
Just make sure you're back
in time to make my supper."

He only ate their kind of food—
Lebanese Mexican
is what she said.

Whatever that was,
Baba ghannouj with corn tortillas
was my ignorant guess.

She took a cab and drove around all night.
She wasn't impressed with Chicago.
(Tame, she said,

Compared to the mega-metropolis octopus of her birth.)
"Remember, *querida*,
I was not some girl from the *pueblo*,

A village *idiota*
wearing *trenzas* and *huaraches*,
who never heard of a diaphragm.

"I used to party all night
over in La Condesa District.
Now there's a city that never sleeps.

"My parents never knew what I did.
I'd say I was studying at my cousin's
and he would sneak me out with him.

"We did drugs together.
We experimented with everything.
When I was married off he cried.

"No one saw him, of course.
He cried in the car.
He cried so hard I said,

"'If you don't stop,
I'll run away.'
'You can't do that,' he said.

"'You have an obligation
to your husband now,
to the family.

"'Don't forget
Allah
is watching you.'

"What
the *chingados* was he talking about?
Was God

"Watching *us*
do ecstasy,
my *primito* and me?

"What hypocrisy!
I tell you."
Lisbeth tapped her acrylic nails on the bar.

She took a belly-dancing job
right away.
But the tips were not enough

To keep
a sick cat alive,
she said.

Then she went to a stripper bar
around Rush Street.
But before

She could end a drug addict
or kill someone,
maybe even herself,

Ni que Dios lo mandaría,
she got out.
The Board Art Guy was

Paying her rent.
Someone else paid
utilities, another for her clothes,

On and on.
Lisbeth could get away with that.
She was wise

About her assets.
And when she went blonde
on a whim or an intelligent guess,

She got a Porsche.
I watched her rise.
I watched her fall.

Meanwhile, I never met the man
who would connect me with the art world.
It's all about timing.

Sometimes you're too anxious,
at others, you wait too long.
It's not always about luck,

Although Lisbeth,
who came from a city where luck
was all most people could count on,

Ran out,
early on.
Her husband eventually

Caught up with her I heard.
It might have only been just
hateful gossip from those

Who also once *chambaed*
at the restaurant.
They said she left me a package.

They saw not only her husband
but two cousins
from Mexico.

No one laid a hand on her
but they put her in the car.
I'd like to think

She might be back in that big house
with the Polish maid
and that one day she'll pick up the phone

And call me.
Some days I imagine
she's back in *El D.F.*

Stoned and dancing up a storm at *Mamá Rumba*.
And still others, I see her
with a child

With her round button eyes
and sable brown ringlets,
pushing a carriage in Chapultepec Park in Polanco.

But that wouldn't be her.
I know she'd rather be dead.
As for the package she left,

It was a manuscript,
four hundred and twenty handwritten pages,
most of it illegible.

Peligrosamente Dichosa,
it's called.
She was too happy to live.

XXIII. Lunar Twin

Put a name to her
so by the curve of her calf,
slope of her hip,

Hollow of her waist,
length of her neck
down to the collarbone

As she turns to you
in her sleep—
you know you exist

Apart from her.
And when María dreams
she has not left

Or died
but only dreams
the dreams of a beautiful woman.

And when she wakes,
slowly, the way
a beautiful woman wakes,

She—
María—not you,
smiles.

Remember that,
you tell yourself,
tho' the temptation of the mirror remains.

"Look at us," she says,
her finger tracing
your leg, slender hip, up

The torso, around your once too-thin
shoulder ten years older
than her too-thin arm,

"We could be sisters," she says,
for the tenth time
since the night before.

But you are not
sisters.
And there are differences

(Thank God)
between you,
subtle as they might be.

"No," you say,
for the tenth time since
last night.

"Your eyes are jadeite,
precious gifts from
the Earth,

"With glints from the Sun,
while mine, obsidian,
that when sharpened,

Become daggers."
(Yes, I actually said
daggers.

But that *was* what our ancestors used
on their victims:
daggers of obsidian.

And she was my victim.
Poor her—
not me—

María,
victim of my clichés.)
She was right.

We did look like sisters.
We were the same height,
had the same ebony hair,

Straight, with pointed ends
like a geisha
gone gothic.

Same nut-color skin.
Even the *china* eyes—
from a receding gene going back

To the Wisconsin Ice, perhaps.
(¡Ay—
China poblana, ven pa' ca.)

Everything about this woman
the same
down to the tapered fingertips,

(Does she have a scar on her left knee, too—
from learning to shave
on the sneak with her mother's rusty razor:

No, of course not.
She is
perfect.)

But no one knows about the scar.
No one looks into our eyes.
And besides these minor incongruencies,

The gods have deemed
to make two
of us.

We could have stood in for each other in a line-up.
"*Ohmigod*, it's so hot in here.
Open the windows, will you?"

She asks, instead
of what she really wants to say—
or at least I do,

Which is: how
do you fall
in love

With yourself—
Remember
what happened to the Queen in *Snow White*?

Blancanieves, not she,
got the prince in the end.
And what about this—

Don't you hate
when a man dares to compare you
with another woman?

Like we came out of factories
with serial numbers and bar codes
to match us up when they needed to replace a part.

Like—
(we say "like" a lot)
Brunettes: Made in New Jersey

Blondes in Orange County—
or else,
Ha, ha. Listen, listen:

We might joke
using the made-up voice of a man
we'd never met

Or met one too many of him.
You must be from Uruguay—
I once dated a woman from Uruguay

And she had a beauty mark right above
her mouth —just like yours.
Yes, it could be funny,

If it wasn't so true how we abhorred
our invisibility in the world,
except how we appeared

As whores.
Not that we did it for money.
Not that we would do it all.

But this country has its traditions, too.
This one would be about seeing
pretty brown women

Like us, me, they, all were at a quadroon ball
hoping to be picked out
and bought

As men's personal acquisitions.
They wouldn't get
the house in Park Forest.

Their children do not attend
Montessori.
No country club memberships

For cleaning women
with fine
asses.

We met—
María and I.
And now we were doing it,

Comparing
todo
down to the sparse hairs

Up in the corners
of inside the thighs.
I got that from my mother,

She was from Morelos—Are you from Morelos?
She looks horrified.
Even with the ten years between us,

With a ceiling mirror
which her bedroom
(Thank God) does not have,

It would be freaky to see us
hands locked, limbs straight out,
Like the paper cut-outs

I made from old newspaper
for my little sisters,
the ones that grew up not to look

A damn bit like me.
And now this
younger woman—

This—
doppelganger—
who slipped through the fifth dimension.

As I feel her lips
cover mine with the same fullness,
Yes—

That before her kisses
were glossy candy-apple red with plum liner,
yes—

Tacky, I know, but she, too,
outlined her lips with a plum shade pencil,
heart-shaped,

The precise fit is almost, tho' not quite,
(thank God)
too much,

Inebriating—
this lunar twin—
as she lifts her body,

Lays it on mine and I think,
this is how my weight
feels,

This heavy or this light,
depending
on how much a lover

Wants you
there.
We have breakfast,

Something simple.
We can't cook.
We can't even think,

Too wrapped up in staring.
At the table, face to face,
if I look left, she looks right.

"Stop it," I say.
"I will not" and she makes a ring,
A loving handcuff,

Around my wrist with her fingers.
Uf. Tiny. Pathetic, she says,
Just like mine.

That's it.
I'm ready to go.
No one

Has a right to unnerve you like this.
All your life
you are nothing

But a hologram
on the street,
a hologram in bed,

Across tables.
You rarely materialize
and when you do

It's not good.
And now this—
Fax marked urgent

That looks nothing
like you at all.
You're sure of it.

Most definitely not
like anyone remotely
related by blood

This one who
people said, "You've got to meet her.
You'll see. The resemblance is…"

At the party
All you thought was
how much you liked her sense of humor

And the two dashes of green
when she almost closed her eyes
taking a puff off your cigar.

And your son,
long asleep—you hoped—after preparing
for a high school entrance exam,

And nothing to keep you
from this woman
and one more dance.

Your brain's gone blank.
The kimono you borrowed
slips open

The silk sash loosens itself,
like *duendes* are around
and in action.

Her kimono comes apart
the same way.
The mimicking stops here,

You say.
She laughs
a beautiful woman's laughter.

Oh—
from deep within,
like a soprano's vocal exercise,

Warm,
claret in color,
a bossa nova on a harp with a bongo beat.

She hangs pictures of herself all around her apartment.
Mirrors on every door.
Not like you.

She's nothing like you.
See?
She has hats,

All styles hung on the living room wall
like an art collection,
but she wears them,

They belong to her.
She belongs
to herself.

You belong
to no one,
which, up to now

Has done you just fine.
I'm leaving,
you say with your eyes.

And you can tell
she understands.
She has the same expression.

Digital graphics.
How many of you will there
be if you stay?

But you don't move
and neither does she—
Until your gaze lands

On the table
in front of the bay window.
"*You paint?*"

You ask
the obvious.
There are brushes and jars and tubes

Worst of all,
a very large watercolor pad,
lying so innocently about.

Then you know,
without a doubt,
that's it.

And before she says,
Don't go.
Or, my boyfriend is away for the weekend,

Let's
hang
out.

You have put on your jeans,
your black sweater,
your boots

(Or maybe they were hers),
and made it out the door,
pushed the elevator button hard,

Pounded it with your fist,
until you realize she has not
come after you.

XXIV. *La Otra*

Are sons born hunters or made?
No matter how gentle or safe the dwelling,
The male child out of necessity

Must venture away as a man.
And she, pleased to know that he was a man,
let him go.

They did not become strangers or friends.
When he came by they sat in the study,
she, stringing beads of sense against

The wreckage of the outside.
Or at least she tried—
not being the conventional

Mother with a simmering stew.
Left on her own
She did not join canasta clubs or learn to play golf.

She did not tutor children or read to the blind.
She'd had enough of children
with the raising of one.

She'd had enough of cleaning offices after dark.
She'd had enough of men who wanted a woman
for the price of a dinner.

She'd had enough
of her own mother's demands
although her mother had been dead a long time.

She'd had enough of the poor altogether,
the working class
and the middle class.

She couldn't have had enough of the rich,
never having been rich and didn't know anyone who was,
but disliked them on principle.

Like everyone else she did know,
and a lot whom she didn't,
she'd had enough of Washington.

So she packed a small bag,
(the same one "the Hunter" had used for summer camp)
and she split.

XXV. A Night Without Stars on the Isthmus

She swallowed the sumptuous neck bone
of a turtle hidden
in *Sandunga* stew.

Sandunga was not an exotic
dish or a spice
but a robust woman,

Skin, the color of bark,
y frondosa
like a leafy tree with a wide trunk,

Mixed-blood Zapotec
born in the Isthmus
of Tehuantepec–

Not mythic but legendary,
for being so real and earthbound.
Sandunga,

Tehuana de mi corazón,
Juchiteca
if she comes from the Village of Juchitán.

The women run the markets.
Their children are the best fed
in the Republic.

They are boisterous,
laden with gold coins on chains and earrings,
bright scarves around their heads like fortune tellers.

But they are not wanderers or of mysterious origin,
But *indígenas—mestizas—*
with everything that passes through that tropical paradise.

They live for the fiestas,
grind corn bare-breasted,
let gay sons wear dresses,

Everyone has a job and a place
and the women
run it.

But—
It isn't true
that they run their men.

The *Sandungas* administrate.
There's a difference,
they insist.

The men don't stay home,
like docile love slaves,
Ulysses, transfixed for seven years.

They fish,
make fireworks,
catch iguanas, spin humongous pots.

They plant and harvest
lots and lots
of indigo—

They turn over their pay to their wives and mothers
before they waste it on drink,
or something just as foolish.

Make no mistake about
la Sandunga's
feminine extravagances,

Satin *enaguas*,
loose hair adorned
with crowns of aromatic blossoms,

As she rides by standing
on the back carriage
of a three-wheeled motorbike,

Not with the air of a queen,
but with the purpose and authority
of Secretary of State.

Oh—so many changes for the ways of
la Sandunga coming up
in the name of progress,

Or as she would say, cutting to the chase:
Ay—
But for a long while,

The older, the fatter,
the more she was praised,
the more she was valued.

Tell me—
what could be wrong with that?
Tell me—if you can,

Those who think of Mexicans
small
of build and height,

Small of mind and ambition,
with no past to build on,
no one to receive them with respect—

Where still they go to work,
have they ever tried
to bargain with a woman from Tehuantepec?

They flirted that night,
Ella y la istmeña—
at the *vela*—

That was a party that lasted 'til dawn.
This one was held in the name of San Blas.
The people of the Isthmus are not

Catholic, so much,
nor were they *pata rajada* pagans,
but who they became centuries down the line.

A red stain
reminder on the forehead—
not Hindu, flower of the trumpet vine or hippy tattoo,

But vestige
of when they were
branded.

Baby girls and wrinkled *doñas*,
rotund and well-formed maidens,
Even a pretty transvestite or two decked out to the nines,

Started off the outside ball without men on the dance floor.
The two women danced all night—
She—

(Who had taken a bus south—south
with her teenage son,
sulking alongside all the way down,

And who had gone back to the hotel
as soon as the fiesta began,
everything so foreign as it was.

(In any case, an adolescent at a social event
accompanied by a mother
never made a happy pair.)

And *la Sandunga*,
upper arms flapping to the rhythm and a firm grip.
They danced with the other women, too.

Each and every one draped like a dark velvet bell,
swaying, swaying
in silks, lace, and thick cloth strips

Wrapped around luscious graying hair;
and flowers abounding,
wilting fast in heavy coastal air.

With a hand on a hip—
They took breaks to fan themselves
and chug down beer after beer,

Feasted on blue *tlayudas*,
desserts of honey-sweetened plums,
smoked their own hand-rolled cigarettes.

Telling jokes with double entendre punchlines.
What excitement among the so-called libertines—
what fare!

Until something sharp
caught
in her throat.

The treacherous bone sent her—
not to where
at the end was a bright light inviting,

Her dead relatives flagging her in
like railroad signal men
but a sublime

And almost immediate
arrival at a place of no return.
Oh—

Not Tamoanchan.
No mortal adult
ever went there.

But the trap door that opened
at the end of all the hells of Mitlan
to complete and utter elimination

Of the *indio* soul—
(those we call
the Aztecs who called themselves by many

Illustrious names in their heyday
but not Aztec.
As the Ancient Greeks did not call themselves

The Ancient Greeks.
While the Romans, on the other hand,
as also the lost tribe of Israel

Still hold their ground
regarding God's intention,
Aztec, therefore, is not used as an archeological excursion

But as a point of reference.)
Where *she* went—
Ella

Llegó ser Dios mismo—
that is—
(Again, get this)

One
with
God's presence.

What God?
Belonging to Whom?
None other

Than
the God
you Imagine.

As everything blacked out with her final breath
She had no doubt
that she had left this life

And entered another.
No one noticed
when she fell

Just as the world has never
Noticed
When she stood.

She fell by the crude wooden table,
like a morsel of *tamal,*
sniffed at by stray dogs, stepped on by dancing feet.

Meanwhile,
(get this once more)
she started the journey of all *jornadas,*

The one most difficult to explain.
To the left of her brain
was the band still hardily playing,

While to the right—
a suction as soft as an inhaled whistle
of Something calling

Calling,
bidding her welcome.
"I'll take her home,"

Her hostess announced—from another stratosphere,
"She's had too much to drink."
and everyone laughed.

She—
could hear the laughter.
Ha, ha, ha,

Or in Spanish,
Ja, ja, ja.
She's drunk.

Está borracha
la gringa.
Yes.

In Southern Mexico
she was of all things,
gringa

But then, *la Sandunga,*
seeing she was not red but had turned white,
stuck a fat finger down her throat

To save
the Watercolor Woman's
life.

"*Ya,*" she said, pulling out the bone,
like a wartime surgeon working
under dire conditions.

She held it up
triumphantly
for everyone to see,

Passed it around.
Yup.
It was a turtle bone all right.

People patted her on the back
and she drank down another
little bottle of beer, so proud of her victory.

(As if it hadn't been her fault to begin with,
leaving that bone in the stew,
Ella—who was slowly returning to consciousness,

Thought to herself.)
But never mind.
No harm done. And what was past soon passed.

They carried her back to *la Sandunga*'s
mud and adobe home,
with the loom for embroidering Chinese flowers

On velvet skirts taking up most of the front room.
And concrete floors dusty from open doors. In the patio
she rested on a hammock covered with a net while

La Sandunga rocked it
like a cradle,
as if no one had a care in the world

That night without stars,
while next to
la Sandunga dichosa,

Was a grandchild at her breast
And at the other,
her happy man.

While *Ella* drifted off
Something stranger happened,
Stranger than even death

And resurrection.
Her paintings,
Crude yet pure expressions of herself,

As they had always been,
came to her head:
one by one—

Click,
click,
click,

Numbered and named,
even alphabetized,
like the works in that art history class

Way back when.
they were all self-portraits.
Not a Frida fetish as a lover once suggested,

(A woman named
Pánfila,
which in and of itself discounted anything she said.

Pánfila was a cowgirl who rode
a giant cockroach with wings.
That had been

Another reason
to get rid of her
fast.)

But this isn't about
tawdry remembrances of things past,
but of almost dying,

Even if just
for a few moments,
on that brief vacation,

For which she had saved
to venture to the land of her ancestors,
to give her half-grown son a sense of himself.

And of women like the Tejuanas,
Juchitecas,
las Sandungas.

She hadn't of course,
worked like a *burra* all year
just to go somewhere to die

So young.
(Everyone thinks of herself
as too young when it comes to dying.)

And with still too much to
what?
She swung, slowly, easily,

Beneath a no moon sky,
drifting off and starting to dream of
her four hundred and two paintings:

Mimixcoa,
she called the collection—
like four hundred stars

In indigo *cielos.*
Count them.
Native peoples of the Americas

Had always revered what came in
fours,
earth, water, air, and fire.

Spring, Summer,
Autumn, Winter.
East, West, North, South.

You get the picture.
If you want to complete the sacred turn,
you add five for the center

Of the universe.
In this case, there were four
plus two more:

Moon Sister
and the jealous brother
with piercing rays

Who slayed her and their four hundred star sibs
each and every dawn: The
Mimixcoa.

Every night they returned
brightly shining,
tenacious as some kin can be.

Moon Sister repaired herself
in a month's time.
Then came back

The *canaya* Brother Sun
rising from the East
to do them in again.

Ella smiling in her half-sleep,
rocking in the welcome breeze
like a ripened fruit on a branch

Made a decision there and then,
But like all major decisions
That catalyze a transformation

Forever after,
This one would take a while before
being implemented.

One must always think these things through.
But not too long
or else they will never happen.

She had died,
she was convinced,
that balmy evening,

And as she had returned,
apparently
it must have been for a reason.

She gave herself one.
She would show the *Mimixcoa.*
She would bring her paintings to the public,

To the *theys* of the world to see and judge
who proclaimed what was what,
and what was definitely not,

She would bring the *Mimixcoa* out,
tho' they might pity
the primitive use of her brush,

Distortion of perspectives—
how she always got one eye too big,
the forehead too narrow or too broad,

The *chata* nose much larger than it was on her face.
She had nothing to hide
or to apologize about.

She had died once
and once was enough
to know she could die

And that would be that,
but she could not return
and live without stars.

XXVI.   Are Hunters Born or Made?

"Born!" Weighed in
la Española at the dinner party.
"We are not animals,"

The South American immediately
Came to his own defense,
"Oh, I beg to differ," his *compadre*,

Who until then, had little interest
in debate was inclined to
to confess.
"Good for you!"

La Española clapped her hands,
"It's refreshing to meet
an honest man."

The hostess—
wanting everyone to go away
as friends

Changed the subject.
"Let's talk about our
children. What universities

Have you picked?" She
asked the South American
whose child was her *ahijada*,

Meaning bonded by baptism.
All their children knew
each other:

Same schools,
summer camps,
foreign student exchange programs.

The son of *la Española*
had taken the daughter of
the South American to the prom.

What a gentleman!
What a lady!
They'd stayed out all night.

That's okay.
That's okay.
That's the tradition

Nowadays. In this country.
Don't worry.
Don't worry.

No pasa nada.
No problem.
What do you think will go on

In the dorms?
Oh, in my day,
my mother thought

I was a virgin until
I married.
Good thing I wasn't.

What an imbecile
my ex-husband was.
¡Qué torpe! ¡Qué bruto!

"No, no," says the hostess,
divorced three years.
"Mine—

"Ugh! I can't even bear
to remember it,
much less speak of it

In mixed company."
"Look,
look," the South American

In polo shirt
and Baum & Mercier sports watch
dabs his mouth

With a napkin, clears his throat,
"Look," he says again,
as if he's caught a stutter

From the topic, "It's not like
I don't think.
It's not like I don't feel."

"Yeah,
yeah,
yeah," says the *compadre*,

Like the fifth Beatle
or as if his friend were a politician
and should never

Be taken seriously.
"You know it
And I know it."

He maintains his position,
and doesn't dab his mouth,
but lets a trace of oyster sauce

Make a half ring along his lower lip.
"We think with our…"
But mindful

Of the opposite sex
as he has been direct,
he does not finish.

"You see!" *la Española*
feels vindicated by at least
one male's agreement.

Apparently
one is better
than none at all.

She bites down hard
on her salad,
chews with vigor.

She is divorced (as are the rest).
She's stunning
like an actress—

Not a Hollywood cut-and-paste,
maybe she is an actress, but bodacious,
without Botox or collagen.

"Born!" She says again crunching romaine,
some hearts of palm
maybe down on an olive pit.

I am putting
in extra time with a catering outfit.
I don't work in the kitchen.

I just serve,
pick up plates.
I overhear things.

She has caught my gaze.
"What do you think?"
She asks.

"*¿Qué piensas?*"
I am not
paid to think,

Obviously. I only smile back.
But in my opinion, if I were to express it,
is that the hostess has been

Too generous
with her guests.
The oysters—

Out of season—
have been flown in.
With her stockbroker husband gone,

Entertaining in a new penthouse
with a twenty-eight-year-old fiancée,
or sailing his yacht to the Fiji Islands,

Or racing in the next Indianapolis 500
where he'll probably
kill himself,

Who is she having to impress now,
or for whose sake?
Who cares about the fashion shows

Or charity work?
Why bother with dinner parties
with men who bore her worse

Than her husband had?
Why not join
a climbing expedition,

A water polo tournament?
A divorced woman
should be able to qualify

For a witness protection program.
Go far
far

Away
and start again.
New passport, color contacts, wig.

Maybe throw in some liposuction. The works.
She smiles at me.
I wish I didn't need

The money.
I wish they hadn't even noticed me,
the way it usually goes.

Liberals.
Surely they've guessed
I speak Spanish.

(Not a stretch
in this business.)
The fact that they do too,

Act as if it bonds
us all
in the U.S.,

If only out of sentiment
and no other import.
After all,

They had servants back home, too,
from whom, in my modest opinion,
I'm sure they did not solicit their opinion.

But here,
they convince themselves,
I have a chance

To jump the fence,
to get ahead,
if I try, if I work hard enough,

If I learn English.
They never stop to think
I may not be

Foreign,
that I am not
foreign at all.

I wish I had a day off,
that I could watch Mars
get closer to Earth

Than it's been in
sixty thousand years.
I wish I were seventy-three

And retired
and able to get drunk on tequila
on my birthday—

As the old ones were permitted
in the days of the Aztecs
without shame—

And tell my children
and my grandchildren
and my great-grandchildren

To take a jump
in the lake.
In Chicago, the Lake

Is pretty big.
I wish
I were the Virgin Mary

Eternally untouched.
I wished my mother
had loved me better.

And that my father
had known what to do
with a daughter,

Like these people, fussing over dessert
and smelling the parfait,
alumni and familiar with academics,

And who know down to the last cent
what college will cost,
for their young ones,

Like I've had to learn
a fuerza
for my son.

I wish a lot of things
standing there holding a tray
with my sore arm over my head,

Ordered to pick up and not
to engage in small talk.
I wish I could die and wake up on Mars.

Not really, but like in a movie,
floating face down
in a swimming pool.

Gurgling an aria
with the throat of
Kiri te Kanawa.

I once loved my boy's father.
He was the hardest working man
I'd known.

I loved him like a brother.
Oh—
And we know

That story so
I had to leave him.
He—

Like *la Española* contends,
eyebrows furrowed
expectant of my reply—

Was a hunter,
a discreet predator,
of the voluptuous and less

Than virtuous.
Oh—
Indeed.

He was convinced because he paid
it wasn't
adulterous.

Blame me, I said.
for leaving him
for a woman.

And he did.
And they did—
I gather up the silverware.

I balance the tray with one hand.
My shoulders aren't
what they used to be.

I say nothing.
Are husbands born or made?
Don't go by me.

Why don't they leave me alone,
ignored as I usually am,
functional in the room,

Like a chair or
like I'd prefer to imagine:
a blurred figure

In the background
of an elaborate fresco,
as if the artist had really not

Planned me out,
which isn't true.
And maybe

Just maybe,
did you ever think about this?
I keep the composition

Balanced,
so the eye won't go off kilter?
I started to think about

Life's voyage
in portraits
a long time ago.

But even Rembrandt would not
have touched the subject.
Maybe Goya.

Picasso was a pig.
Still
everyone worships him.

No one worships
the model of Botticelli's Venus.
Who was she?

What am I getting at?
Only that it's time to go
bring out the coffee,

And not lament
with these ladies.
If they knew a woman

Once broke my heart,
they really wouldn't respect my opinion.
They might even throw me out.

That's how deep
gynophobia goes—
a woman pities a woman

Who doesn't have a man,
even if
she's lesbian.

Everyone thinks
it's not out of choice
when women love each other.

I loved her.
That didn't make me a lesbian.
She found my g-spot

Each and every time
for years.
That made me

A lesbian.
I want to put the tray down,
sit and hold *la Española*'s hand.

Not because I find her
attractive
but to comfort her.

It is the world
we have been given,
I'd like to say.

It is the life we have.
Let's make the best of it.
I might one day love a man.

But like Gandhi said
when asked what he thought
of Western Civilization—

That it would be a good idea—
I might one day love a man
if I ever find one.

XXVII. Mistress of Death

When the earth opened
y me tragó la tierra
he, who would not love us

Not me,
not her,
when he burst forth in a black chariot,

Four black horses
carried us down
to where I would not love him.

And he would not care,
and made me his queen.
Hades is not at all what people think.

There were vineyards
with luscious green grapes.
All the peasants from the countryside

Came to make white wine.
There followed enormous festivities
that went on for weeks.

He put me in charge of manufacturing
and promotion. I designed the label:
A Watercolor Woman bathing

In the fires of hell.
Something like
El alma en purgatorio

Only smiling,
like the Chiquita Banana logo
of the United Fruit Company.

It sold immensely, especially
in the United States and France.
Germany was skeptical.

The Turks were having a recession
and stuck to their own libations.
Speaking of which, I ran into poor Çamal,

The lover with the sheep and cows
and the marvelous mouth, who
was killed at war.

He didn't deserve to be in hell.
We didn't speak.
My lover grew fangs the size of rhinoceros horns

The moment another man
got next to me.
It goes without saying

I did not want to be there.
My pets were two wolves,
One on each side.

One night I stayed awake
brewing up a plan for escape.
I became very Machiavellian.

I would tell him that while I did not want
to leave the three-legged nymphs,
the eunuchs with giraffe necks,

I'd had word that my mother was ill.
Yes, the dead one.
(He knew she was dead.)

But everything gets turned around
in Hades.
He was so demanding,

Was and, surely, remains.
Such a devil in disguise,
he even confuses himself.

He finally gave me permission.
Yes,
that was the worst of it,

Having to ask permission.
Well, no.
The worst could have been any number of barbarities

A woman was subject to by a sinister
Sin vergüenza,
a devil is truly

A despicable presence
only welcome in the Underworld.
The worst was not the sneering

When he'd had too much to drink.
The worst might have been sodomy,
The only way *el Diablo* copulates.

No, the worst was
there was no
exit sign anywhere.

"You may go," he finally granted,
after giving the matter some thought.
Still, I knew he suspected

Something was off.
"But you must come back in spring."
(In hell it was winter all year long.)

"*Sí, amore!*" I said, "*Sí, sí, sí!*"
He mulled it over some more.
One night he called me to his *cantina*.

Hades was sharpening a tool
used for cutting grapes off the vine.
It looked like a small sickle.

My wolves were with me.
I started to tremble. Without realizing
It, I was twisting the animals' ears.

They weren't trembling.
They were standing very still.
"Please,

Don't kill me,"
I begged for my life.
"Tell me why," he demanded,

Without looking at me,
but went on sharpening
the blade.

"*Ti amo,*" I lied.
"*Ci vediamo nella primavera,*"
Finally, he gave in.

He took me for a real dolt.
Of course.
He thought with his dick.

He ruled with his dick.
It was his scepter, barometer,
his God.

And Woman, by virtue of not having one,
was simply,
nothing.

Nevertheless, the next morning he gave the word
and gates that were not there before manifested.
His mother, whole clan, the rest of the thousands

Of earless, eyeless minions,
who never questioned
what had been for eons, opened the locks.

They wept like goats as I left
stocked with enough food to last a year,
prosciutto, cheeses, café,

His mother's homemade gnocchi,
truffles, two gallons of wine,
and two large Coke bottles

Of our special virgin olive oil
that I hadn't gotten around to
marketing.

I was weeping, too,
for those left behind and
out of relief for myself.

And of course, because Hades
had not been so bad,
except for him.

In spring, when the trees began to bud
in Chicago, after the long winter and
tremendous snow storms that fell

Right after my return,
there came a wailing,
the entire city heard.

Oh—
Louder than a fire engine siren,
more chilling than the howling of wild dogs.

It was he—
Hades crying
like an old widow

Crying inconsolably,
Over she,
who got away.

XXVIII. Between the Aztecs' Pyramids and the Ancient Egyptians'

Another version of the long journey to the far away:
This one did not include women who died for love,
although laws being what they were,

One man threatened to leap off a balcony
after making love to a woman who was not
his wife. But she would be no one's wife,

And no one's mother again.
In the *ahwas* she smoked a *sheesha*
with apple tobacco and listened

To verses that resonated gold,
like bushels of saffron in the market,
overflowing with hibiscus flowers and cumin seeds,

Digging deep her hands
and still without end of their abundance.
The only laments and the only regrets

Were the memories lost to what had never been.
Ella no contaba lo triste.
(And neither will I.)

Ali wanted her as his third wife
and Lydia, as her companion.
Prayers resounded from the minarets

Permeating the Cairene air.
In her soul to calm her from above
cleaved Saint Claire—the violent dove.

She fits now and belongs to nowhere—
Ella, who the devil left for dead.
She and I sleep together,

Whether on sacks of wheat or a proper bed.
We sleep the sleep of *Xochiquetzal*
in *Tamoanchan*

Who is all flowers and song,
and dreams of her Rain God.
Tlaloc, furiously calling,

Stomps through the clouds
with thunder and torrents.
Xochiquetzal dreams

Of two beings who met beneath
the *Tonacatcuhtli* Tree
and painted her in their image from

An eternal moment of longing
for the Divine,
not to be One or to challenge deities,

But to escape the relentless agony
of the uninhabited heart,
in this life or in any other.

XXIX. The Fields

Let's talk about the fields
at the end of that year, at the end of her life.
Let's talk about the cows,

The black and white ones,
those that grazed along the Aegean.
What?

Did you think I was still on this continent?
In this country that calls itself a nation,
that bangs and bends the world with its

Mighty might?
Did you think I was possibly talking
about cows in Texas?

No.
I meant the ones by the ancient bluest of seas
near Ephesus, across from their nearby brothers of Greece.

Yes, me,
I am talking,
the ghost of the brown woman.

A lover came to her/me/us there
and made a bed of yellow grass
and brittle hay,

A canopy for shade of palm fronds.
The roar of the waves before tide.
In the distance

The cowbells for a serenade
and sheep crying to be led home.
Right then, hell was no longer.

The lover, an Anatolian, would fight the Kurds,
not of his own will, of course,
when he'd take two bullets to the chest.

But that afternoon, he looked up
from between her legs,

and asked why there were women who didn't
Like to orgasm.
And she threw her head back and laughed,
never having known one.

He laughed too
and fed her mulberries, plump as sweet bugs,
dripping red down her chin.

And that was a day
to make anyone want
to visit Earth again.

But something has to be said
of the cows left behind in Texas,
if only as a postscript,

A mention of the heifers in particular.
Let's see.
But what can be said of heifers grazing

Spoiled as they are,
with udders that hang so low
and long for so much.

Wishing their hooves could extend
themselves to catch silver moonlight,
but never can?

What may be said of the row of lovers
that came and went even until that last season
of her travels?

How mortality bore a more intoxicating scent than
jasmine? How no woman may refuse
to be possessed

And left at peace?
But neither were the rest.
A moment of silence

Then,
for the almost-seductress
who cracked her skull on a Harley-Davidson,

For Lucca, who took all the pills when he
woke up alone in a *pensión*,
for the drunken journalist who talked too much

And wrote too little,
for another drunken journalist who talked too much
and wrote too little,

The anorexic princess who fell
with one of Isis's tears
and sails forever on the Florida Keys.

The mature socialite at another port waiting
with a single rose,
and for good measure, the handsome nephew

Of a carpet seller who,
on his twenty-fifth birthday
was also stood up.

Ella escribió su propia elegía.
It's not at all what anyone wants to do.
As if one could without premeditation.

But we can—she and I.
the one left to remember
and the one free to die.

XXX. Splendor and Obsession

A woman was once
my splendor.
At other times, males

My obsession.
Someone once told me
(probably my mother)

That to have and hold
a man
meant everything.

Yes,
that was
my mother.

And her mother
before
her.

And on
And on.
Yet there is that braid

In the trunk,
along with other secrets
Mamá Grande felt safe

Sharing three generations
of women down.
The abundant

Virgin
hair of my childhood,
like a trousseau in a hope chest,

That goes off with the girl—
who will not marry—
but would prefer to join the circus.

So far I have hung on to it
and have not had to sell
that or any other part of me

To get here.
Here, meaning the present
and in one piece

Safe,
healthy, and well-nourished,
as is my son.

I come from people
who still think
of success

As having
enough
to eat.

But my son
spared of war and famine,
poverties untold

And desertions,
may be
hunter in name only

So much to conquer
without definition or form
at near-twenty,

He doesn't know where
or how to begin,
starting with

One's sense of self.
Are hunters born or made
is not the only question.

But equally provocative:
does the prey
have a chance

To get away unscathed?
I have
worked for years

Carving out
the narrowest of paths,
un caminito de apenas,

An inch at a time
with the tiniest instruments,
the crudest of tools,

Available:
a toothpick,
baby spoon,

Hairpin,
paperclip,
fingernails, teeth,

For myself
to pass through
with my child in tow,

Who having passed
through me
was my obligation

And part of my soul.
(I threw out
all my books on

Existentialism
when I became a mother.)
It did not matter

His gender.
Oh—
He was mine

And a part of me
forever
and always.

Are men born or made
hunters—
And do dykes

Pretend?
Hush, girl.
Shush, woman.

You know better.
No I don't.
Not she.

Not I.
Words are a curse
when they cease to ask

Questions
and insist on a response.
Worse, the one you want,

Not the one you get.
Forget
the sterile reductionism

Of economic laws.
Or dare I recall
the romance Feminism

Had with Simone who, tho'
more brilliant than
her men,

Deferred to their egos.
Intelligence alone makes not
the champion javelin thrower

But endurance, strength of mind,
ability to calculate distance.
It doesn't come to everybody.

Most fall short
of one gift
or another.

So that was how
Elvira was left
in the grip of the supervisor

She didn't want to go.
Or, as she put it,
where would she,

Where lack of documents
would not cause
her more trouble.

I took up
odds-and-ends work,
all related

To the service industry,
which has an abundance
of openings

Rotating like a ferris wheel
only faster,
for the people in the margins—

Not the homeless.
Not those on medication,
or government aid,

Not the degreed,
the too-proud-to-get
their-hands-dirty,

The just-not-that-needy.
But me.
I did catering,

Baked sweet breads at 2 a.m.
in a *panadería,*
took the elderly

To doctors' appointments.
Things like that.
One day I had saved

The cash
for my ticket
out.

(I never believed
in plastic.)
One day

She and I were not
just packed and ready to go
(we'd been *that* for a long time)

But were actually
in a cab riding to the airport.
She let out a laugh

I'd never heard before.
She was talking
and acting in ways

I didn't recognize.
She could've been
la viuda alegre

Like *tía* Renata,
or the saloon girl
that Mamá Grande

Had been a century before,
so gay was she
and with that errant laugh

Like a new pair of shoes,
stilettos with lace-ups
around the ankles,

She had the laugh of the wicked
woman—
delicious and brash,

Wilful and petulant—
at her age,
just imagine.

How I began to envy her.
until I understood,
just about the time

We strapped on our seat belts,
first-class, of course,
that she was me and had always been.

Glossary

cazador de corazones   Hunter of hearts.

Chalchiuhtlicue (in the Aztec-Mexican pantheon)   "She of the Jade Skirt," an Aztec goddess of baptism, storms, streams, rivers, and seas.

Chilangos   Long-term residents or natives of Mexico City.

Cipactli (in the Aztec-Mexican pantheon)   A primeval sea monster of indefinite gender.

Compañero, bien Pos-Sandinista   An activist in the post-Sandanista period.

Conscientización   Left-leaning political consciousness that motivates action.

Ehécatl (in the Aztec-Mexican pantheon)   The god of wind; also, one of the creation gods.

el hijo   The son.

Ella   She.

files   Agricultural fields.

Indio   Person indigenous to the Americas.

Iztapalapa   Borough of Mexico City.

la Otra   The other.

maquiladora   A sweatshop established in Latin America, particularly common along the border with the United States; also, a woman who works in the sweatshop.

Mamita   Mommy.

mestizo   Term used for a person of mixed racial background who is native to the Americas.

Mictlan (in the Aztec-Mexican pantheon)   The land of the dead; where the dead go.

Mimixcoa (in the Aztec-Mexican pantheon)   The "four hundred" (innumerable) stars of the North.

Ometecutli and *Omecihuatl* (in the Aztec-Mexican pantheon)   A pair of gods who represent duality and the primordial forces of nature.

peligrosamente dichosa   A dangerously happy woman.

Quetzal   A bird native to the highlands of Mesoamerica that was highly prized in pre-Hispanic culture for its turquoise plumes.

Renacimiento   Rebirth.

Sandunga   A waltz native to the Tehuantepec region of Mexico; also, a woman from this region.

Tamoanchan (in pre-Hispanic Aztec-Mexican religion)   A mythical green paradise, believed to be a place of origin; birthplace of Xochiquetzal, the goddess of beauty.

Tezcatlipoca (in the Aztec-Mexican pantheon)   "Lord of the Smoking Mirror." His name is a reference to the obsidian mirrors used in divination by Aztec priests.

tía and *tío*   Aunt and uncle.

Tlaloc (in the Aztec-Mexican pantheon)   The god of rain.

Tlaloques (in the Aztec-Mexican pantheon)   Tlaloc's four helpers, who resided on hills and mountains.

Tonacatecuhtli (in the Aztec-Mexican pantheon)   "Lord of Our Sustenance." A creator god who was associated with fertility. He was often depicted as a tree.

Tonalli (in pre-Hispanic Aztec-Mexican religion)   One of the three souls with which a person is born; also the animal day-sign that accompanies a person on the day of birth.

Xochiquetzal (in the Aztec-Mexican pantheon)   The young goddess of love and beauty.

Xolotl (in the Aztec-Mexican pantheon)   A grotesque, doglike god related to sickness and death. *Xolotl* resides in the underworld of Mictlan.

READER'S GUIDE

1. Recount Ella's life story. What are the major events that take place in her life, according to this novel?

2. In the early pages of the novel, we are introduced to several of Ella's family members: her parents (the "Lord and Lady of Sustenance"), her great-grandmother Mamá Grande, her brother, and her aunt. How do each of these individuals help to shape Ella into the person that she becomes?

3. Why does Ella turn to painting, and what meaning does painting hold for her? When you imagine her artwork, what other artists come to mind?

4. The novel focuses heavily on the daily living conditions of migrant workers and their families, beginning with Ella's parents' arrival as part of the Bracero Program. What are some of the specific concerns that Castillo raises? How do these societal concerns shift over the course of Ella's life, and how might Ella evaluate society's progress on this front?

5. How does mythology operate in the text, and what role does it play in Ella's life?

6. How does Castillo's use of the poetic form enhance or complicate your understanding of the novel?

7. What does the title of the book mean to you? What makes someone watercolor or opaque? How might an opaque person transform into one of watercolor?

Suggested Readings

The Mexican Revolution
The Mexican Revolution figures prominently in chapter 4, "Mamá Grande."

Knight, Alan. "The Mexican Revolution." *History Today* 30, no. 5 (1980): 28–34. Accessed February 10, 2016. http://www.history-today.com/alan-knight/mexican-revolution.

"The Mexican Revolution: November 20, 1910." *EDSITEment!* (blog). The National Endowment for the Humanities. Accessed February 10, 2016. http://edsitement.neh.gov/feature/mexican-revolution-november-20th-1910.

The Bracero Program
See chapter 3, "Lord and Lady of Sustenance."

Bittersweet Harvest: The Bracero Program, 1942–1964. The Smithsonian National Museum of American History. Accessed February 10, 2016. http://americanhistory.si.edu/bracero/introduction.

United Farm Workers and César Chávez
See chapter 9, "*Renacimiento* (or, Death to All Dwarf Roosters Who Think They Can Fly)."

"The Rise of the UFW." United Farm Workers. Accessed February 10, 2016. http://www.ufw.org/_page.php?menu=research&inc=history/03.html.

Maquiladoras and Femicide
See chapter 17, "In the Jaws of *Xolotl.*"

Hampton, Elaine, and Anay Palomeque de Carillo. *Anay's Will to Learn: A Woman's Education in the Shadow of the Maquiladoras.* Austin: University of Texas Press, 2013.

Nieves, Evelyn. "To Work and Die in Juarez." *Mother Jones*, May/ June 2002. Accessed February 10, 2016. http://www.mother-jones.com/politics/2002/05/work-and-die-juarez.

Contemporary Border Crossings and Migrant Workers (1990s and 2000s)

See chapter 16, "*Tonalli*."

Holmes, Seth. *Fresh Fruit, Broken Bodies: Migrant Farmworkers in the United States.* Berkeley: University of California Press, 2013.

Invisible Victims: Migrants on the Move in Mexico. London: Amnesty International, 2010. Accessed February 10, 2016. http://www.amnestyusa.org/sites/default/files/amr410142010eng.pdf.

Latina Feminism

Charleswell, Cherise. "Latina Feminism: National and Transnational Perspectives." The Hampton Institute. http://www.hamptoninstitution.org/latina-feminism.html.

Gallardo, Susana L. "Issues & Ideas." Making Face, Making Soul: A Chicana Feminist Website. Last modified October 5, 2011. http://chicanas.com/issues.htm.

Mythology

Cartwright, Mark. "Amazon." Ancient History Encyclopedia. Last modified October 22, 2012. http://www.ancient.eu/amazon/.

———. "Aztec Civilization." Ancient History Encyclopedia. Last modified February 26, 2014. http://www.ancient.eu/Aztec_Civilization/.

Miller, Mary Ellen and Karl A. Taube. *The Gods and Symbols of Ancient Mexico and the Maya: An Illustrated Dictionary of Mesoamerican Religion.* New York: Thames and Hudson, 1993.